THE

TELEPATHS

OF

NEW ORLEANS

by

JJ LEANDER

ANTISOCIAL TENDENCIES

The first time I felt it, I wrote it off as being a stray daydream. The sort of fleeting thought that seems bizarre, apropos of nothing. After all, I was taking a little vacation in the middle of a work week. An experiment with working the night shift was paying off during my hunting hours.

Mount Wachusett was not just a hill and looked to me like it was set far enough apart from the city to be empty wilderness, unpopulated woodland. At least I had hoped it would: instead, there were major disappointments waiting for me.

The uphill hike was a little more than I had bargained for, and I was out of breath when I arrived at the peak. Then it was an unpleasant surprise to learn I was not alone.

There were couples and small families scattered over the hillside, all facing west. They were bathed in a soft golden glow. I hiked away from them and tried to find a spot where I could be by myself and out of earshot.

Temptation shouldn't spoil my moment of peaceful contemplation.

As it was, only the most rugged rocks were unoccupied, leaving me to choose a grassy spot. The sign at the beginning of the climb had warned about the rocks and grass being perfect habitat for snakes, including venomous ones.

It gave helpful hints, should we "disturb" the rightful owners of the mountain.

It seemed to me that snakes and other hill dwellers would prefer to avoid the squatters, and visitors would need to do little. The predators would likely wait for everyone to leave, then check around for the smaller animals that usually clean up the crumbs and popcorn left by sightseers.

I selected a spot covered with pebbles and only a little greenery. Still a hazard, but certainly a lot more comfortable than the flinty rocks that remained after the tourists claimed the conveniently smoothed boulders.

Then I became one with the other golden-faced watchers, as we waited for the brief glory that was sunset over the wetlands. I thought we must look like artwork. Impressionists might paint the reflecting ponds and oddly broken paths of the natural walkways. The reservoir and its environs spread out below us, where even the mucky swamplands became beautiful as the sun set.

Despite the chattering people fixated on the patterns of color and light, a few raptors flew around the wetlands, occasionally venturing overhead, perhaps looking for snacks.

Soon it would be too dark to hunt, and they would go hungry for the night. Or maybe they, too, would wait for the rabble to leave, then hunt before the darkness became complete.

I wondered if a hawk or vulture would gladly pick off even a poisonous snake and find some ingenious way to kill its prey. Or just gobble it alive and writhing.

The feeling hit again.

The first chill had been how I wished I could just make all the people disappear. Was I willing to create havoc, or attack someone and watch the others run to protect their families?

Even the worst, ugliest thoughts pass in an instant, and I could fight my way back to normal.

This time I felt okay with the crowd, comfortably apart as I was. They had lost their voices when the sun touched the horizon, making all the gold turn to coral red.

My favorite color. Why would a red color be named coral? The only corals I had ever seen were white, and even dark ebony colored.

I personally had never seen red coral. Of course, I had viewed programs where scuba divers used their search lights on the reefs, but even then, coral was not red. Not in those shots. The clownfish wore the bright colors, and the octopuses would change to match their surroundings, but they didn't turn red.

My musings were interrupted by a sudden pain in my eyes. I shut them but still could see the setting sun.

Great. Probably burned my retinas. I glanced around and the people were still watching, rapt and appreciatively cooing and murmuring. If I looked slightly askew from them, I could still see faces and clothing. Otherwise, there was just the bright burn of the sun, and it changed to bluish-green when I closed my eyes again.

Once again, I hated them all. Why were they so easily enthralled by what was practically a daily, or nightly, occurrence? And they were teaching their children to love the sun, and the earth, and the sky!

As if it were their entitlement, their birthright!

I wanted to sweep those people off the hillside and send them plunging towards the sunset. They loved it so much, let them have it.

Probably couldn't hurl them far enough to even reach to the end of the atmosphere, much less to the sun itself. I snorted at the absurdity of thinking of being able to hurl them at all.

Where had I gotten such a notion?

Oh, I know it's not normal for civilized people to imagine extinguishing the lives of others. Mind you, I feel only loving acceptance of the world's lower animals. I could never harm the most vicious of large predators, either.

After all, humans are simply highest on the planet's food chain. We can easily kill and eat even the great cats that terrorize their prey on the savannahs around the world.

Personally, I always felt more kinship with the hunters in the forests, especially those that stalked the night. It's a shame I cannot afford to hop a flight to Africa or South America. The jungle seems just the place for me.

I hadn't done it yet, but more and more I wanted to start a little killing spree all my own. I would begin small, perhaps a homeless person here and there, then work my way up to the mostly forgotten poor, and aged loners.

No one would miss them, and I would be doing everyone a favor. Single living on the margin of society, is a hardscrabble life. Especially in the United States of America, where the rest of the citizens are keeping more and more to themselves, avoiding the company of others, particularly strangers.

Eventually I could prey on small families, maybe a single parent and some young ones. It would be easy to find them, also on the outskirts of daily middle-class culture.

A few might be grateful if I worked quickly. I would pick those who were mired in poverty, and already preying on one another. It is no trick at all to find and sometimes befriend them.

I could put up with their company, knowing that I would soon end their suffering. An angel of death: no one to fear.

EARLY YEARS

The small, nuclear households felt familiar to me. We used to live day by day, with no future to speak of, except suffering, hunger, and the undying wish to escape the open prison of our place in society.

Even my mother was relieved when a do-gooder reported our entire household to the authorities. We children were removed from her care and she went to jail for child abuse and criminal neglect and more.

We kids were separated and placed in foster homes. I understand my twin made out very well, adopted and assured of a good future. We lost touch after I went into the State Hospital for Children. Never heard from her again.

Neither of us ever tried to reconnect. I despised her almost as much as we hated our mother, so it was mutual all around. We had managed a sort of truce, about a year before the State stepped in. We simply stopped speaking to each other.

If there were food available, we ate singly. If not, we went our separate ways to forage. Mostly we stole from dumpsters, where we also managed to find clothes. If a real windfall should appear, we would sneak through the alleys of the inner city, looking for others like ourselves. There we could barter whatever we had for what we needed.

That's how we got caught, one day that seemed to begin like any other. We had gone out to scrounge and barter, and to pimp for our mother.

My sister wasn't especially clever, or maybe she just deliberately got careless. She thought she had found a client for Mommie; what we all got was an under-cover cop who wouldn't do business with Abby. He simply found our home and went in to "woo our mother" for the next hour.

That was a lie. People are good at lying, especially undercover cops.

My sister and I were collected from the schoolyard, where we usually went while she entertained a client. We were surprised, but not upset.

Never saw Mommie alive again and didn't bother to find where my twin wound up. The foster system gave me information about them just once. I told them not to trouble me with any further news, and they had to comply.

There was never a group home created that could comfortably hold me. People weren't the problem, ex-cept when the home had to send me for counselling. At that point, I knew I had overdone it and dialed back a few notches to being just a sullen throwaway kid. The next assignment would last a little longer.

Not thieving, not running amok, yet I knew I scared the hell out of them.

Fine. Their fear pleased me, or rather, it *tasted* good.

Being in foster care meant that I had to go to school, where I chose to remain an outsider. Report cards meant nothing to me, and I managed to bump along from one grade to the next.

It seemed smart not to antagonize anyone, and that proved my perfect formula. Just as it had been with our mother, I was left alone if I didn't cause trouble.

I was under the impression that there was something about my mother that didn't settle too well with the fostering parents. No one told me what the problem was, but there were only a few people who would deal with me, usually some outsider, unfamiliar with our part of town.

That was okay, because I could do more without causing trouble.

What sort of trouble? Well, I didn't really know. I thought I was handling things properly, going along at a steady but neutral pace. Day by day I performed for the teachers, guardians, and counselors, right up until I was placed in the UMass Medical School Pediatric Hospital.

So much for staying out of trouble.

There was little change in my lifestyle at the UMass facility by Lake Quinsigamond, except that the counselling got somewhat intense, at least for my therapists. The social workers came and went. I could tell they were despairing over my "detachment," as they called it.

Right up to the time the psychiatrist prescribed antidepressant drugs. The only effect I could sense was a nearly permanent, emotional separation from others. It was a contented dullness that left me feeling a bit brighter and freed me from the usual requirement to attend classes and group activities.

The drugs kept coming, along with a few memorable trips for electro-convulsive shock therapy, in a clinic way over on the other side of town, near Greenhill Park.

The food was better at the adult facilities.

Maybe it only tasted better because they made me fast before the treatments. Otherwise, after they administered the general anesthetic, I simply went to sleep. They were the only times I did not dream.

Usually my sleep is filled with pulsing chaos, looming unnamed danger, or some deadly peril, so the treatments were welcome. Eventually they stopped the ECTs, and I was pronounced cured.

Whatever that meant. I went into a halfway house, where I was taught to keep myself presentable and healthy, and how to manage among supposedly normal people.

That's all I learned while I lived among similar throwaways who also did not give a damn one way or another. Without exception, we were eager to qualify for release into general society, where we could revert to our usual selves.

That was the big prize, but there were other perks. I even went to a special needs high school, where they allowed me to take classes that stressed future work. There was a hint that they were preparing me for the real world.

It had taken five years of being shuffled around from one home to another, then to UMass Pediatric, and finally graduation from the halfway house. It felt to me like a victory, finally being shoved out of the system. In fact, I had simply reached legal adulthood.

There was what I called a ¾-way house that took in people like me. We all puttered in a sheltered workshop, where we were encouraged to learn a trade. I asked to work in cooking, preferably in a cafeteria setting.

I didn't plan to spend years learning to become a chef. I just imagined using the knives to take out my aggression on already dead animals.

PROFESSIONAL STUDENT

Cooking worked well for me. I had never learned to make anything in my childhood. It was gratifying to be able to create something that was essential, not just useful.

The satisfaction lasted until I got good at it. Then I was invited to watch the lunch crowd, sucking in all the food I had worked on. In less than twenty minutes, everything that took hours to prepare was gone, either eaten or tossed into the garbage.

Into the garbage!

The hatred boiled up inside me. They were disgusting, the way they would lean back and sigh, or even happily belch. Then they went out of the cafeteria, leaving behind a huge mess.

After the diners were gone, we cooks were also expected to clean up. I didn't mind it before I watched the eaters, but afterwards, I wanted to vomit when I had to collect whatever they tasted and left behind. Then I was forced to throw away my own handiwork.

Regardless, I persevered.

If nothing else, it gave me a few evening hours when I could wander around the city of Worcester, to see how other folks existed. Apparently a lot of them lived very well, indeed. It was a lesson that would serve me nicely later.

In the poorer neighborhoods I found more identifiable sights: messy yards, ramshackle homes, and subsidized housing. It fascinated me that some of the units in the projects were immaculate, right next to slummy ones. That image, too, I filed away for future reference.

In a couple of years, the food service supervisors declared me an excellent cook, and the boss spoke to my counsellors—three by then—to convince them I ought to be encouraged to become a chef.

They told me it would be a huge step up, that I would eventually make a lot of money and might conceivably become somewhat famous.

Fame: the last thing I wanted, but I was intrigued about the possibility of riches. With enough wealth, I could do whatever I pleased. With money comes respectability, and no one would suspect my extra-curricular activities, which had become considerable, both in time and satisfaction.

A day of drudgery in the kitchen would reap a round of prowling in the wee hours. More alone time than I ever had. It felt a little isolating, but occasionally I would meet another nightwalker like myself. I began to experience a new sensation.

Other folks have an amazing abundance of feelings.

My family had only hate and fear. Also, my mother often complained about loss of her lover so long ago. Most of my new acquaintances were just as unhappy, but they felt other things, too. They were wide-ranging in their minds, and I started to feel *their* emotions. It was a completely novel enjoyment for me, and new people brought gratification like I had never known.

It was a wonderful way to spend a night before returning home to sleep a few hours before my job. Working at least filled my days.

A quick student, I was willing to go the extra mile. No task was too boring; no challenge beyond me, in my quest for the prize.

Eventually I won a fully paid admission into *Le Cordon Bleu*. Rather than bother to learn a new language, I enrolled in the London school, and found myself among a delightfully different type of people.

It made for more interesting evenings. In London, a lot of citizens walked outdoors at night. It was a truly cosmopolitan city, and I had never known such freedom.

It took nine months of almost around-the-clock studying and laboratory work to earn the certificate. They wanted me to remain for the Bachelor's in Food Service Management, but it was laughable to envision myself as such a specialist.

I only wanted to siphon feelings from people, even at the expense of their sanity. As much as I detested every person I ever met, I didn't do physical harm. However, neither did it bother me when I later realized that some of their psyches were depleted or destroyed.

More than one man approached me with some unholy sexual assault in mind; I left them babbling idiots. They didn't or couldn't suspect that I might be the stronger one. I guessed that I looked like an easy touch.

I was not an easy touch. In fact, I didn't have to *touch* any of my filthy, hardly civilized, victims at all. Just as soon as they came close, I could sense their feelings, even the ungodly horrors they planned for me. They were just as obvious as their physical stench. Then I just sort of drew in the stink along with their evil feelings.

In self-defense, I learned to seek out individuals from better neighborhoods. The younger ones were thrill-seeking, and I gave them much more than they bargained for. They didn't get to kill or rape me; instead, I was able to drain them. It wasn't an even exchange, but they got what they deserved.

It was soon obvious to me that my prowling did not go unnoticed. I was tailed by local police who were interested in my activities.

Fortunately, I had not fully engaged in my hobby, and no one was killed. The constables simply stopped me in the alleys and told me to go home.

It was *dangerous* wandering in the night like that.

I humbly thanked each officer and changed my route on the next excursion. That worked for only a few weeks. After a while, there was nowhere I could go to be my predatory self.

My solution was to apply for an Associate's degree at *Le Cordon Bleu* in Miami, Florida. With the honors I had earned in London, it was easy to attain a full scholarship, with work-study at one of the best restaurants in the area.

CULINARY SUCCESS

By the time I earned the degree, I realized that the only advantage I got from Miami was somewhat more comfortable weather. I had erroneously expected it to be drier than London. On the contrary, other than moist, warm nights, there were also a few horribly humid ones that sucked the life out of my prey, ruining the game.

On top of that, rather than gain a new venue for my hobby, I found myself the victim of several muggings. Once I dispatched the easily confused criminal, it was difficult to find a place to dump the body, so I just left them where they lay.

What's the matter with Miamians? They were very much into body image, and even the nearly psychotic delinquents seemed to be posers performing for whomever they met. Usually connected to gangs, some were simply unlucky drug addicts looking to support their habits.

There is little sport in further twisting an already ruined mind, whether drug-addled or just inside an empty head. It was a quick drain-and-dump, leaving a quivering victim or unconscious drug addict.

After a while, I felt I needed a little more challenge. A change of local color, at least.

Having given up on Miami, I used my degree and certifications and applied to the New Orleans Culinary Institute.

Once, again, I had all I needed to apply, with plenty of money to fill in the holes caused by a decided dearth of grants. In little time, I was practically on my way to the Mississippi Delta.

Physically getting there was going to be a long haul, because there had to be a stop in Atlanta, Georgia. There was no direct land route and only the intercity buses would take me anywhere, each requiring a transfer for the leg to New Orleans.

The usual temptation almost won; it would be tempting to thumb a ride up to the Florida panhandle, then over the shoreline route to the Big Easy. I could think of things to amuse myself during—and between—rides.

My target town's nickname did not apply to arrival and departure. On the other hand, the opportunity to mentally torture victims while hitchhiking was a lure I fought mightily to resist.

Instead, I opted for a quick hop by air. It was cheap and I had a pleasantly short time watching out the window. The plane was full of hilariously excited partiers, anticipating the night life. I hoped it was a preview of opportunities that waited in the Mississippi Delta.

The Institute was not really interested in me, not enough to award a grant, and they were otherwise at capacity. There were so many would-be chefs clamoring to learn the latest fads that popped up on a nearly daily basis in the food preparation industry in that city.

No problem: I simply rented a place in a part of town with plenty of after-hours foot traffic and began to prowl.

My previous schooling had set me up to take my pick of day work. What's more, the restaurateurs were fighting for me—actually bidding against each other for my night hours.

It would be stupid to name where I finally settled in. You may have run across me on my way to and from work, but my name and face remain fortunately anonymous in the kitchen. As usual, I was able to completely detach myself from coworkers and even the owner, who was slightly disconcerted by my lack of interest in his cooking style and clientele.

Since I was willing to work long hours, my skills soon dispelled any qualms he may have felt about me. After that, he gave me all the time I needed to rest. I did not rest, but instead prowled around the city, avoiding some creepy people who thought they were Dracula-type immortals.

The more I tried to hide, the more those local characters pursued me. For the first time in my life, I felt stalked. The nighttime vibe in the city was strangely disturbing.

Nevertheless, I managed to soldier on. New Orleans was a challenge. The cemeteries literally called to me—their living occupants, that is. I was especially drawn to a richly adorned grave that seemed to have an unending parade of visitors.

Silly Goths just wanted to show off for their tight circles of friends, leaving me without a kill on many nights. I began to hunt in what were essentially ne-glected, ancient family plots. They were usually empty of the living, but here and there, I would find an alcoholic that was just enjoying a place to drink cheap wine and sleep.

They made my best targets. If they were still awake and aware of their surroundings, I could practice what had become an art for me. I really earned my reward with those drunks; they would react to my overtures, but often lost interest when I didn't drink with them.

Not to mention that they were practically tapped out, emotionally, by the time they stumbled into the burial grounds.

I did have one rewarding encounter on what had to be a historical property. The already intoxicated victim was lamenting the old days and her past friends. She seemed too aged to be still kicking, let alone drinking.

The old woman startled me when she initiated the en-counter.

She called me Sweetie and asked if I wanted some champagne. I nodded and moved in, but she was way ahead of me. She flamboyantly popped one of those new, brightly colored replacement corks and held out a magnum of Dom Perignon.

I sneered.

"Pretty expensive stuff for sloshing, don't you think?" She cursed at me and said she could drink whatever she wanted.

"Nice attitude for such fancy tastes, Lady. You must have been something else in your day." That's when she got a bit snotty and began regaling me with tales of her earlier glory.

I knocked down each of her pretty pictures by comparing them with her current state. She had owned the property but lost it through failure to pay taxes; she had to feed what had become a multiple-substance habit. Now the city owned her old manor, and no one wanted to purchase what was reputedly a haunted house.

"I don't detect any lost souls, except your own, woman."

There were no real haunts in the place, just a lot of history that tended to replay itself. The old girl was accustomed to the apparitions and willingly stayed as long as she could.

"And you live here now, so to speak?" In answer, she sneered back at me. She could use the place because no one bought it.

And then I understood. *She* was the haunt. Chuckling, I slipped the bottle from her hands and sucked out enough to fizz up my mouth. When I swallowed, it was a good reminder of why I don't drink alcohol.

That's a human thing, along with a variety of other disgusting habits involving natural intoxicants found worldwide. This individual would not be missed; her self-involvement reminded me of myself. No one on the planet was looking for me, either.

I took her hands and looked into her eyes.

"Are you lonely, little lady? Where is your family?" No family left, not in New Orleans. I began to draw out her memories, savoring her self-pity and anger at those who abandoned her.

Murmuring softly, I agreed with her assessment of her current, sad state and encouraged her to continue. Her mind was already half-gone, but I confused it further with comments decrying her terrible relatives and how unjustly she had been treated by the municipal government.

In only a little time, she was ready for the reaping. She began to curse everyone and everything around her in that "God-forsaken" town. All the while, I agreed with her random assessments of every evil thing that occurred around her. Then I pounced.

In a honeyed voice dripping with false empathy, I asked her who was to blame for it all? Surely she could point the finger. Whom did she want to kill, or at least bring down to her own level?

Of course, it was about *everybody*. No one had any respect for a genteel lady anymore! She was even approached by the Chamber of Commerce. They suggested that she should offer her place for tourists, advertising a haunted house, and play the scary owner!

She began to moan. One moment she was furious that *they* were content to let the place go to ruins. The next she whined that she was the victim of dishonorable city elders. Finally, overtaken with anguish, she cursed everyone around her and even God Himself, for letting all the bad fall on her head.

And she was mine. I drained her, blissfully soaking in all the sadness and self-pity. It felt good and turned out to be the best meal I had had in months.

To hell with Miami: too much of a fun, feel-good philosophy. So up-and-coming, with the melding of cultures and the ever-mixing sexual tension. There was just so much energy that it was self-perpetuating. No one really deserved all that fulfillment and fun.

No, indeed. I had just found Utopia.

New Orleans was my new city.

BLOWBACK

It took a few days, but my feast finally made the round of local news. Not that anybody could guess how the old lady died. No, the news was all about the rise and fall of a great neighborhood dynasty and their mansion.

The coroner was mystified at the post-mortem. There did not seem to be enough alcohol damage or other deterioration in the body to indicate a cause of death. And so, *natural causes* went on the certificate.

After a whole day of reading every newspaper tsk-tsk over how tragic it all was, I was satisfied that there must be an unending supply of such encounters. Of course, I would have to search them out, and be a little more careful in my choices of prey *and* locations.

Never did find another perfect blend of sad-sack circumstances and convenient red-herring as that formerly wealthy alcoholic, but I was content that a little extra effort and patience would pay off.

What's more, New Orleans was the perfect place to find such fallen aristocracy, at least, those who considered themselves as such.

The best part was that they were conveniently situated in largely deserted neighborhoods that were also full of visibly run-down estates with sprawling properties. Oddly enough, my victims did not even question my presence.

Thus began my midweek excursions through the un-advertised sections of New Orleans. There was no lack of drug- and alcohol-addicted humanity to enjoy. Each had a wonderful story about how badly they were treated by all the snobs and do-gooders among them.

Heart-breaking stories of alienation and mental abuse filled those encounters. It took little skill to pump up their wells of self-pity and regret.

Regret is more satisfying than self-pity, but beggars can't be choosers. I would have to start my own little humanity farm and plant it with the dregs of fallen high-society stars to enjoy the former.

Even that carried a heavy load of risk. In New Orleans, twenty-four hours of every day was filled with opportunities to purchase illegal drugs and party. And a large police force worked hard to counteract it.

My first hurdle was to separate the day-trippers from the natives. Few people would travel to New Orleans just to forget about life. Tourists are not generally good prospects for negativity.

Except perhaps the idle rich, but even they would dress down and move among the rest of the vacationers.

One Wednesday night I took a chance and visited the grave of a famous Voodoo Queen, hoping to flush out some of the underbelly of the local populace. If bad luck were the only criterion, that cemetery would be a bonanza for the likes of me.

Unfortunately for local tourism, there were other predators in the burial grounds. They were also assessing the visitors but only wanted their money and jewelry. I waited for them to attack a few targets, and when they were satisfied with their haul, I would intercept them on their way out the gate.

Icing on the cake! They would find the exit least likely to be used by sightseers and local law enforcement. First, I would pass close to see if they were interested in a loner. This also gave me the opportunity to scan their mental health and personal attitude.

No one can begin to imagine the darkness in the depths of the miserable, criminal soul. It did me good after all the slap-happy Miamians.

I learned to mentally mark a few and follow them, one by one, to see their next stops. Many would immediately take their ill-gotten gains directly to their personal drug dealers, who were only too happy to divest them of the easy money.

It was sometimes a difficult choice between the pitiful junkie or the equally pathetic supplier. One delicious evening I managed to hunt down both, enjoying a lovely, full ingestion of misery, followed up later with a self-satisfied clown who had convinced himself that he was providing a much-needed service to humanity.

The irony was lost on them, of course, that they would later treat themselves to the same dose of wretchedness as they were doling to other unfortunates.

Stupid people.

New Orleans kept me satisfied for months.

UNINVITED GUEST

Right away, I must admit that the encounter was not by chance. My mother sought me out, having never found me during her lifetime.

She apparently got religion in her last detention. Must have had a lot of time on her hands. I am not a big follower of prison conversion tales, because I have been smart enough to avoid incarceration, and never met a true believer before that night.

Finally, just when I got pleasantly settled into my day and night routine in the suburbs, not far from the hunting grounds around City Park, Mommie showed up to again badger me about my lifestyle.

After a long, sweaty day in the restaurant kitchen, I had done a little prowling with no luck. People don't seem to like hot, humid nights, which I supposed was to be expected. The steamy evenings hindered me in Miami, but it didn't bother me in New Orleans. The game expected such weather and plodded along, despite their discomfort. That night must have been a lot muggier than usual.

No luck. I reluctantly wandered back to my rented apartment.

There was no point in buying property, regardless of my comfortable financial position. Between the hurricanes and the flooding after nearly every storm, it wouldn't pay to own, and constantly rehabilitate, a home in my adopted city.

One can, however, get a genuinely nice rental for the right price. There are plenty of ratty-looking old places that are well-maintained inside. Not particularly picturesque, but more than just livable.

My building even had an old-fashioned, open-ironwork elevator. The landlady was obsessive about the antiques in her place and managed to keep it in good working order.

The other renters were very friendly with her, but she gave me my privacy, probably because I rented the attic. Sure, it got hot up there, but there were skylights that could prop open in the heat and seal shut in the rain.

The night of the paranormal occurrence was signaled by something odd in my apartment. I was accustomed to walking around in the relative darkness after hunting into the wee hours, so it was just by chance that I noticed a bit of light that flashed in a skylight as I neared the gate.

There was no possibility that I had left anything on. It had been broad daylight when I went to work. The landlady charged for all utilities and kept accurate records. It was a little joke between us that I used very little electricity. She even seemed impressed that I didn't want cable on the television.

When would I have time to watch it? Usually, I bought the local newspapers to see if any of my prey were listed as missing persons.

A fortunately rare occurrence.

As for air conditioning: when well-fed on my victims, I felt only satiety, a pleasure relatively unaffected by ambient weather.

This trip I used the stairs. If there were a burglar or other ne'er-do-well poking around, I wanted to surprise them. It took extra minutes and a lot of energy that I couldn't afford to waste, to sneak silently up to my apartment.

The door was locked, but a real criminal with any smarts could come down through a skylight. I knew I might lose them when the key clicked in the lock, but by then it wouldn't matter. I would coax them back and recoup on what had been a wasted hunting trip.

Once inside, I felt let down and perplexed. Where was the burglar? There was nothing and no one in my place. After I checked around every nook, looked at the untouched skylights, and into the lone closet, I gave up and dressed for bed.

No sooner had I slipped in between the sheets, when a soft voice called my name. Impossible! There had been nobody anywhere in my apartment.

I eagerly opened my eyes, only to find what looked like a glowing cloud at the foot of my bed. The phantom spoke my name, her voice making me sit upright.

"Holy crap! Mommie, is that you? So you finally died. Did you ever manage to stay out of jail?" I had no trouble believing in ghosts, especially while living in New Orleans. Then she became clearly visible.

My mother managed to get herself murdered in prison. She had finally begun to recognize the loser she was but continued what she was good at: bitching. I remembered her carping at me, day after day, when we were kids. Apparently, her final time she graduated to being a verbal bully to adults.

She was giving a fellow inmate an ill-advised lecture on the joys of a moral life and good conscience. Of all things for such a woman!

"So, you got God? Hah! Then you mouthed off to the wrong inmate?"

She never could keep her opinion to herself. Even in the heyday of her whoredom, she used to lecture us on how we should live our lives.

"What is it now? Am I going to be visited by three ghosts to convert me? It's not even Christmastime, Mommie, and here we prefer to do the whole Mardi Gras thing instead."

I never knew that ghosts could sigh, but she did—audibly. She was trying to tell me that my immortal soul hung in the balance and was found wanting. Seriously, it was something like that, just not in those words.

"Bingo, Mommie! My immortal soul wants someone's emotions to feast on tonight. Pretty slim pickings during these suffocatingly steamy evenings.

"Don't waste your ectoplasmic breath on me, lady. I am good with going to Hell; just getting in some practice before the Grim Reaper comes to deliver me to my master. At least I will arrive with a decent re-sumé."

Mommie wanted to come clean to me about the circumstances of my birth. She would explain my lust for misery. I wasn't having any of it: it was too late for true confessions. Irritated, I told her to go away.

She obediently faded into the darkness.

So she got God. Well, good for her. Why not? As far as I knew, she never killed anyone on purpose, or even by accident. Anyway, I never asked, and neither did my sister. We would have gotten a dreadful whipping if we had dared.

Yeah, Mommie would have no problem with beating us, especially me, within an inch of our lives. It would have taken little extra effort for her to complete the job. That was part of what put her in prison in the first place.

Later, I found myself wondering if that was her only trip to the state pen, rather than county jail, but by then she was long gone.

Oh, well: there probably would be further visits.

I will say this: even dead, she looked surprisingly good for a change. She was always a mess and stunk to high heavens at least half the time. No wonder she sent us out to shill for her; no one would approach her willingly in the street.

But that night I was glad she left. My only regret was not taking her out myself. Bet her little lifetime of crime and vice would have made for choice feasting.

MORTAL VAMPIRE

This sort of thing—my hobby—doesn't just happen. Living vampires are made, not killed. Mommie had tried to explain about my father, but I didn't want to know. I was what I was, and I had adapted well. As far as I knew, when I die, that will be the end of it.

If you can manage to distance yourself from other peoples' bad energy, it becomes a palpable thing most would avoid, something nasty, almost solid. Then you might be able to feed on it. Lots of abuse victims eventually learn to shut out their own feelings. When they do finally get help, they are put back in touch with their emotions.

That's just the opposite of my story. I knew I loathed everyone from my youngest years. You all just disgust me. If I weren't being paid for this memoir, I could not be bothered to enlighten anyone with my observations.

Somehow, there was somebody eagerly waiting to feed on my bad habit. That should have been the first clue. The publisher told me that readers will pay to be frightened half to death.

If I had my way, you would be frightened to death, period.

My interest in you, dear reader, is not monetary. It's personal. I love your evil voyeurism and want to take it into myself.

Ingesting other peoples' psychic energy is better than eating or drinking, or even sex. Of course that last pleasure may have already been ruined for me in childhood by a neighborhood pedophile.

In my prime: that's how I view myself, although lately, I am not sure how old I am, physically or mentally. And no, I don't think I will live forever. I don't believe anybody does. Blood sucking vampires do exist, but they are mortal.

Nothing that comes from Nature is immortal. Even the planet must eventually die. Then where would all the "immortals" go?

No. It is just a depressing world full of miserable creatures. The lucky ones exist to kill and eat others, from the highest predators down to the plant-eating game species.

Mankind has gotten exceptionally good at it. But still, there is a lot of waste.

That is where I come in. I don't know if I am a product of evolution or de-volution. As I noted above, it doesn't matter to me. It's possible that my mother or sister are like me, but in Mommie's case, it's moot.

Perhaps I should have listened to her little lecture. At the time I wanted sleep and looked forward to my next victim.

The more emotional feasting I do, the less I need material nutrition. It reminds me of times when I exercised too much and couldn't look at food. Only it's better, much more satisfying.

You can imagine how revolting working in a restaurant is for me. If I didn't get to slice and dice meats, it would be utter agony. The best part is when I get to run pork and beef through the grinder.

Directly, I would never be able to kill those innocent animals. Instead, I imagine the meats as human flesh.

Sometimes I try to scent out customers that patronize our restaurant. Often they remain nearby, looking for lesser known historical gems that might dot the area. Perhaps someday my flat in City Park will be just such a tourist draw.

That is, if I am ever caught and destroyed. So far, I have been lucky enough to disable a peace officer before he could bring me to justice. He survived; I left him just addled enough to wonder if he'd had a psychotic episode.

Justice? For whom? I am, after all, just feeding myself. Why should I be punished for draining weaker prey? I would love to find an emotionally robust individual that I could keep alive and visit from time to time.

Unfortunately, most people appear to lose their mind or senses—whatever it is that keeps brain and consciousness connected—by the time I have finished feeding.

Mommie's drop-in rattled me a little. Who would have thought that I could be tracked down by the newly dead? Did she also visit with my sister, wherever she might be?

And is my sister, my genetically identical twin, also a psychic vampire? I doubt it, if only because she would easily trace me, compared to what must have been a real quest for Mommie. And why would our mother decide she must talk to me at all?

She must have come to gloat. She never showed any compassion before, nor did she ever connect with me any of the times, presumably, that she was paroled from the Correction System.

As a result, I spent the better part of my next day off experimenting with trying to mentally connect with my sister. Curiosity was getting the best of me, and I didn't like the feeling. I had been content with my routine of work, hunting, feeding and rest.

A whole day was wasted before I surrendered, bored nearly to death. I could only hope that she was block-ing me, as opposed to being deceased.

As a consolation, the next day I learned the emotional effort was not completely wasted. While I didn't find my sister, I did manage to accidentally lure a victim. My mind was still half-searching on my way to work, and I came across an individual who seemed to be musing on his bad luck.

He was a scout for publishing. His business had dried up, time and time again, over the years for many rea-sons. Between the tropical storms, hurricanes, floods, etc., and despite the advent of a renewed interest in the supernatural, his company could not compete with the larger publishers.

The immediate result was that he was mired in a per-manent blue funk as he watched his life's labor taper off.

As a matter of fact, he seemed more than thrilled to catch me stalking him. When I began the little emotional dance that is the setup for my feeding, it clicked in his mind that the attack could be a windfall.

As his unhappiness evaporated, I lost interest and was trying to decide whether I had to get rid of him. That alone was enough to send him into an elated state: he figured he was saved!

Business-wise.

"Oh, yeah? Well, what if we just clip your newly-sprouted wings and I take your emotions while you struggle to survive?" The fellow admitted that he would prefer to make a deal with me.

"Forget it! I detest your kind and prefer to *drain* you."

That's when Henri introduced himself and pointed out that he already had what he called *my number*. At least, he figured he knew what or who I was. I could listen to his proposition or I could kill him.

He amused me when he promised that I would miss out on a goldmine of willing victims. As a publisher, he liked the idea that I was telling a different story than all the others. He could see that I was not a vampire.

I broke in to inform him that I was indeed a vampire, or wasn't he paying attention?

He pointed out that I was just not the usual blood drinker, nor Medieval Gothic. He asked me if I thought I was immortal.

"Do I look immortal to you? I am starving and could die, even as we chit-chat like this!" A little dramatic, I admit, but I was trying to get him going along a more negative trajectory. Henri wasn't convinced.

He said I didn't look like death warmed over. Either I was exaggerating, or already practicing my craft on him.

Gutsy bastard, but he had my attention, especially referring to my craft. It would do no good to pursue him as food.

Then, I slapped my forehead.

"Food! I have no business looking to feed right now. I have to go to work." That said, I moved away as quickly as I could. I barely arrived on time for my shift in the kitchen.

My supervisor told me I looked as if I had seen a ghost. I smiled.

"No. He was, and still is, alive."

I shouldn't have smiled. Boss wanted to know if I had a boyfriend. Then he had the gall to whisper that he had figured I was asexual.

This was not a conversation that I cared to pursue. I went into the kitchen and began my usual evening preparations. We had a decent night, considering that there was no local festival going at the time.

That was okay. Celebrations irked the hell out of me, because we would have temporary hirelings. They just get in the way and present no feeding opportunities.

Early on, I had learned not to drain the help. We needed them and they were no good to us dead or even emotionally numb. And while they hardly understood what I had done to them, they did view me with healthy suspicion after an encounter.

Nor did I encourage friendships with my regular coworkers. Makes no sense to chat with the people I hate the most in the world. I could watch them, laughing and happy, and immediately feel the familiar loathing; it practically creeps me out.

Fortunately, few waiters and cooks wanted anything to do with me. The owner once told me they didn't like me, didn't trust me, and wished I would go away or die.

Good. The feeling was mutual, except that I would gladly assist anyone on their way out. And not just the door. I kept my ear to the ground for any low-level worker who might quit or be fired.

You can't imagine the delightful taste of shock and anxiety! Even more so with young people who haven't yet learned to work their way through misfortune; they go into a tailspin that hangs around them as they leave.

NEW ASSOCIATES

At the end of my shift, my recent acquaintance met me at the back door of the restaurant. The sight of his amiable, wholesome face disheartened me.

"They didn't chase you away? What do you want now?"

Not in the least put off by my dismissal of him and his offer, Henri smiled and shrugged. He still wanted my story.

I caved in, hoping to scare him away with a few demands.

"You want my story? You'll have to meet me in a safe place. I am not taking you home with me. I don't fully believe *your* story."

He indicated that his place was near the Fairgrounds, within walking distance.

"Look, buddy, uh, Henri, I have to get some sustenance before we transact any business. I am depleted from searching for my family.

"And no, I don't think my family is anything like me."

Would edible food do? He had plenty in his flat. I might as well trust him because we were so close to his home.

"Okay, but if you are lying, or I cannot eat whatever it is you think you've got, then you know who is going to be on the menu."

He said he was good with that. We walked quickly through the middle-class neighborhoods that were situated in patches between all the racing-related businesses around the fairgrounds.

In a building that was no better-looking than my own home, he strode up to the front door and waved a card over a reader. We went in and climbed two flights up to a single loft apartment door. Same card, same sort of reader, and we were inside a brightly lit, airy efficiency set with room dividers near the windows to give some privacy.

Henri went straight to the kitchenette and nuked the remains of a lobster-tail plate with crusty fried oysters. Not terribly fond of oysters, I was still able to suck out enough lobster meat to warm my insides.

A glass of wine appeared at my place setting, and I nearly jumped up in surprise.

"Dammit! You almost got yourself killed, my man. I forgot about you."

It was careless to let him in on that little secret, since he might be able to use it against me in the future. I am not always on top of things when feeding. Too late, I figured, and sniffed the wine.

"Local? Not bad. Thanks for the snack. Not to be rude, but maybe you should tell me a little more about yourself and your company."

Henri said he was the totality of his little editorial company; his apartment was his office. He had begun small, working with local students. He could publish their writing for next to nothing, since they were un-knowns and glad to have their stories told.

All copy was sent to a small printshop run by his family, who had remained in the city after the devastation caused by Katrina. Before that, it had been a staple for local businesses and advertisers. After the hurricane, the presses were cleaned and repaired. Except for the occasional clod of dried mud that would fall out when the presses started, things began to return to normal.

However, Hurricane Katrina had also broken up his family. Most of them lit out for higher ground and never returned. The remainder were his closest kin, and they all supported each other with whatever they could scrape up.

In New Orleans, the paranormal, witches, voodoo and hoodoo and the like, never went out of style. Whatever they could reprint without stepping on the authors' toes, they reproduced in original form. Whenever possible, they created an eye-catching, somewhat lurid cover, and printed the editions as something found in forgotten archives.

They were barely managing to keep the printshop open, with Henri acting as producer and editor-in-chief. On paper, all the family members were listed as partners, financial officers, or whatever would work to placate the IRS.

It wasn't anything that was totally new to me, and I nodded my approval as he recited his narrative of family, disaster, and perseverance. It didn't matter to me if it were factual, as long as he truly had a complete publishing house, small as it might be.

I needed to know it was a legal entity, and not just some fantasy on paper, or worse, all in his mind.

Authoring the story was going to be my job. I wasn't up for doing anything in the shop; I had no intention of quitting my night job. But neither did I want to go to jail for fraudulent business practices, and I sure as hell didn't want any attention drawn to me that might interfere with my hunting.

"Okay, Henri, it all sounds legit, but I want to see your brick-and-mortar works. Take me to your printshop and show me your family's holdings." He looked a little startled, and a whole lot distrustful. I waved away any objections.

"Just want to see if it is up and working. I have been places in my time where they were just a front, and no real business to show."

Still wary, Henri wanted to know if I could give him a little for his family at the shop. Just a short narrative of one of my encounters?

After a bitter laugh, I got annoyed.

"You dragged me here. You had the great idea. You provide me some proof. Otherwise, I will literally take it out of your hide. And nobody would be the wiser."

He pondered the problem for a few moments and proposed that I go with him on a meet-and-greet. If I wanted, I could pretend to be his girlfriend.

I answered with a wisecrack.

"Brother, your family is going to wonder how you got so hard up, dragging me with you to the family shop!" It made me smile to imagine stocky Frenchie Henri, squiring a tall, skinny chef from a hole-in-the-wall restaurant.

He grabbed me—again nearly getting himself killed—and turned me towards an ornate full-length mirror. He wanted me to see that I looked normal. Didn't I know how I looked?

"Why should I know, or for that matter, worry about my looks? I take care that I am clean enough to work in a kitchen, and my face doesn't count for much when I hunt." I noted with pleasure that Henri reacted to that last word.

He then pointed out my eyes: even to me there seemed to be a sort of deadness in them. Why, I looked just like a young Goth chick! I fit the part, especially with my northern city accent. Just a touch of the outsider, he said.

Like it or not, he had a point. We went to the family printshop. Photocopiers and small, color printers were in the store-front, with a larger press running out back, making the whole place vibrate.

Henri introduced me in an affected Cajun accent to two guys about his age and an older woman. For their part, they narrowed their eyes when they looked at me. I had to stifle any urge to size them up as a meal and must have come off as completely uninterested.

He then insisted that I had a story that was perfect for their readers. The idea of a living, breathing, and mortal vampire left them shaking their heads.

Sounded like a crime story; did I have the credentials to write about crime?

I thought about all the work it costs me to track down a prospective victim, then properly prepare them emotionally, and finally to cover my tracks after a meal. I said I had some practical experience.

At that point, I felt an unpleasant ping on my radar. This time, the only female in the place stepped right up to me.

What did I know about vampires? In all truthfulness, I admitted that I knew nothing about sucking blood, flying up to rooftops or moving fast enough that I couldn't be tracked.

The woman was a bit older than me, not exactly an old lady, but surely the matriarch of them all. She did not trust me, but I was certain that she was overestimating me as something nefarious.

"Ma'am, look. I am not a criminal, and I don't carry a weapon, even in the back streets here. Which is where I live, by the way. I can go out in the sun and I don't have to sleep in a coffin!

"So, lady, what else do you want to know?"

She narrowed her eyes again, and although I didn't see it happen, I was sure she was mentally sniffing me. She knew something was off.

So, I was not a criminal? I nearly answered, "Not yet!" Instead I stressed that I enjoy my privacy and keep to myself.

I began to dislike her. She knew something; she felt something. I had to remember that Cajuns trace their heritage back to France. Perhaps her ancestors had been witches, the sorts that were essentially innocuous herbal healers, but still may have had mystical power.

Henri must have recognized trouble on the way, and he began to steer me out the door. He offered apologies and said we were headed back to his place. If they needed anything, they could call.

As soon as we were out of sight and earshot, he crossly turned on me, accusing me of sabotaging his plans. Didn't I know that they could prevent the whole deal from going through?

"Hey, I am not the one with the Wicca antennae!" Henri snorted and told me that none of them had antennae, and they were not Wiccan.

"But you don't deny that at least that lady has some sort of ESP?"

At that, he started to blather about how everybody has some sort of ESP, and that just maybe we had connected with each other. Was it his fault that I never asked him about how he found me?

"Give me a break! Do you mean to tell me that you deliberately connected by telepathy with me before we met face-to-face?" At that point I was irked, put off by the possibility that he (and the older lady) might have read my mind.

It did not take a mind-reader to figure out why my new associate was so annoyed. Perhaps even he could tell I was lying about the criminality of it all. Then he appeared to change his mind.

It was not good to be on the defensive against a possible empath or other clairvoyant. I could feel my face harden and my own eyes narrow with suspicion.

With an indulgent chuckle, Henri apologized for neglecting to inform me of their abilities. Or didn't I think that publishers of the occult and paranormal should know something about their books?

Now, that struck me as entirely reasonable. Much more sensible than my own taste for downed-out emotions.

"So, my friend, did I blow the deal? I have never been much good with people. I am a loner, and with good reason. Agreed?"

Henri gave me a rueful smile and said he would keep me away from the printshop for a while. I would eventually need to learn to get along with Tatie, as he called her.

And then it struck me that I had not been introduced to anybody there. For that matter, Henri never asked my name. I wondered about the rest of my personal information.

He cut into my thoughts by telling me that my personal history and lifestyle were safe with him. He couldn't guarantee anything about Tatie and the others.

"And what was with the fake Cajun accent?" He said it was his first, true accent; New Orleans was his city, hence the Cajun. He only settled back into it with family, and sometimes for show with local business associates.

For the first time in many months, I felt vulnerable and wary. All this could bring nothing but trouble.

And I was stuck in an agreement that I didn't dare breach.

MORE VISITORS

We decided that a small writing sample would make a good teaser for advertising.

I tried to give him the description of our meeting, but he laughed and said that it had already been done. He did, however, become interested in my sister. It would certainly spice up the story if we could locate her and learn her doings.

"Henri, if Abby wanted me to find her, I am sure she would have shown up by now."

Henri gave me a piercing look. He shook his head. Then he asked me if perhaps I thought my "sister" was just a construct of my own mind.

"Henri, I would know if my identical twin were an imaginary friend! Why would you even think that? I had messages from the Social Services while we were both in the system. We grew up together before the State intervened."

He backed off but continued to probe my mind, and I exploded.

"Hey! Knock it off! That's fucking intrusive, just like your Tatie! And why don't you believe me? Henri, I think your head is still full of ideas for stories. Go write your own; you don't need me! I sure as hell don't need you."

Disgusted, I tried to walk past him into the hallway, causing him to try to coax me back. He reminded me that we had an agreement.

"Don't start that shit with me, buddy. If anything, I could take you to court for harassment. Legally, you have nothing on me."

He stiffened and seriously threatened to turn me in for murder.

And I just laughed. How on Earth could anyone connect me with the deaths? Even the coroner was stymied.

However, from then on, I would remember to keep my hands to myself, and refrain from touching my victims. I told him so and left.

My bed never felt so good as it did after that unsettling business. I was sure that whole clan would prefer to let this sleeping dog lie.

Nevertheless, there was an unfamiliar humming on the wall that woke me in the morning. It took a while for me to remember that I needed to "buzz-in" any visitors. Never had any before that day. I hit the TALK button on the console.

"Yeah? Who is it and what do you want?" I had told no one of my address.

The oddest voice crooned at me that she was "my" Tatie.

Oh, shit. I really kicked a hornet's nest with that printshop!

"What do you want?" Just to talk. I sighed, told her to take the elevator, and I buzzed her in. Then I listened as the creaking machinery worked its way up through the center of the building.

Tatie stood at my door, patiently waiting for me to acknowledge her arrival. The scent of the predator was now in my nose, and I very reluctantly let her into the apartment.

"Good morning, I guess, Tatie. Talk to me." I showed her to an upholstered chair and sat on the sofa. She was taking in the whole place from the floors to the skylights.

I was certain she was testing me, trying to trip me into a burst of anger.

"Again, woman: what do you want?"

First, she wanted some coffee, and after all, wasn't it time for breakfast?

"You must know that I eat little, and breakfast is for early risers. I work late afternoon to early morning. Breakfast, Continental or otherwise, is not part of my repertory."

In response, Tatie stood up and waltzed into my kitchenette. Without hesitation, she opened a cupboard and found some instant coffee that I didn't remember was there. Then she put on the kettle and took out a mug. She returned to the chair.

"Make yourself at home, why don't you?" At that, she just smiled. Then she scolded me for my bad manners. After all, I invited her in and that made her my guest.

"Tatie, I don't do guests. This is my haven away from people." All of whom I hate: she finished the sentence for me. I scrutinized her emotions but found nothing malicious.

For the first time since I arrived in New Orleans, I felt a shock of gut-wrenching fear. This woman could block my abilities, and I had invited her into my home!

It is well-known among paranormal dabblers that once the Devil has been invited into a home, he could stay as long as he desired.

No, not a devil, she admitted, but she needed to see for herself that *I* was not demonic. I felt a pang of distress, as one who feels the police moving in on the hideout.

"You can see for yourself that I am human, and I swear that I am mortal. My own mother recently died, so I expect I will, too. Now, if you are satisfied, I suggest you finish making your coffee and take it with you out the door."

But Tatie was not done with me.

Her given name was Mercedes, and I could call her Tatie. No, she was not a Wiccan, nor a Satanist. She was non-practicing.

"Non-practicing what? Santeria? Voodoo...?" She drew back and seemed to need a moment to recompose herself. Of course not! Those were all religions arriving in corrupted form from Africa paganism and further jumbled in the Caribbean before they came to NOLA.

That was the first time I had heard a person specifically say NOLA as one word. Before, I had only read it in advertising and the news. Mercedes would use it often, rather than refer to our town, city, or whatever.

And who would have guessed that I had stumbled upon a real, old-school Cajun enclave? After all, while I understood that there were many Catholic people in New Orleans, it seemed to me they were just minding their own business.

"So, Mercedes, what is it you practice?" According to my guest, she practiced prehistoric Christianity. Never heard of it; was it a *thing*?

They were all a family of telepaths, including those who deserted NOLA after Hurricane Katrina. Henri was indeed her nephew, along with the other men from the printshop.

She wanted to know why I lied about my criminal activities.

"I don't consider them criminal. Just hunting trips that may or may not result in some nourishment. I don't deliberately kill anyone; there are simply weaker individuals who cannot accept the lessening of their anguish. After all, I only drink in suffering. Theoretically..."

You only *help* those who want to be delivered from their wretchedness. She again finished my sentence. And she was not buying my defense.

"And you want...what? You didn't come all this way to spend quality time with me, or to check out the furnishing and décor."

No, she allowed that she wanted something specific from me. I kept my mouth shut and tried to listen without expectation.

Her first concern was that I leave Henri and the others alone. Nodding my head, I was able to agree with her. I knew what she meant: after all, Henri and his relatives were not my prey.

"Actually, Henri sought me out and wants me to write for him. I didn't know about your family abilities. When you think about it, he probably could just skim my mind and take it from there. Why trouble me to provide the details?"

She informed me that I was very naïve. How could I not know that I reeked of evil, that I was an easily recognizable predator? My very soul already did not belong to this world. Coming to NOLA was likely the first step towards my own irrevocable ruin.

I sighed and told her not to worry about me. My mother had already stopped in on her way to whatever was her reward or punishment. And I hadn't really believed in ghosts before then. So I was good with whatever came next.

Once more she seemed to meditate then muttered something about the *Archange Michel*. Even in French, I could detect a plea for deliverance. So I knew I must be a bad guy in her books.

Even so, she did not seem the least bit afraid of me.

"Look, Mercedes, do you want me to back out of the deal? Would you like me to move away and pretend I never met you and your little coven?"

At that, she grinned, showing perfect teeth. If anyone looked dangerous to me, the little woman fit the bill.

The buzzer sounded again, ticking me off.

"Look what you've done! I bet you've dragged your nephew here. I never wanted him to know where my place was. Nor anybody else, for that matter. What are you trying to do to me?"

I punched the button on the wall.

"If you are Henri, what do you want?" I barked into the console, but I already knew who was there, so I buzzed him in. He climbed the stairs and arrived almost by magic, he was so quiet and quick.

Tatie seemed angry. She berated Henri for following her and warned him away from me. For his part, little Frenchie said I was everybody's concern. And so they went back and forth, obviously jockeying for control of the situation.

I settled on the sofa and enjoyed the sparring. Apparently not all was peaceful in their little publishing house. In fact, if I let them keep at it, they might make a decent, two-course meal.

No sooner had I thought it, then both stopped arguing and turned to me. I shrugged.

"Well, what did you expect? I tune into unhappiness! It is my sustenance."

Sidelong looks between the two cued me to their thoughts. Of course I was the evil one, and they must have felt like avengers, out to stop my predation on God's people in New Orleans.

"So let me get this straight. You are telepaths who run a publishing house? Okay, would you like to tell me just what has happened to all your contributors?" I leaned back on the cushions, and smugly waited for their response. I knew the answer, just by their re-action.

Both Henri and his Tatie were brought up short and cleared their thoughts and emotions.

"Guys, if you've come here to dissuade me from my feeding, you might as well get out right now. I have a right to the emotions I drink! And when you get down to brass tacks, I am doing no harm at all. Most of my victims are loners who have lost everything and turned themselves into the miserable creatures that I find and eliminate.

"In my hunting grounds, only the resilient survive long enough to escape. I cannot kill the strong-minded, or stout of heart, if you will.

"So let me ask once again. I want to know just what happened to your earlier contributors."

Of course, they were dead! All the books they cur-rently printed and sold were left to them by the au-thors. Each novelette had been written about moving on to the next world, for the New Agers who love the occult and satanic or angelic.

"And? Come on, people. I am not stupid. You must have assisted them in their quest for the other world or other side or portal, or whatever." Now I knew I had their full attention.

On the other hand, I didn't detect a mean bone in Mercedes' or Henri's body. So I didn't think they could kill anyone.

What the hell was up with them?

From my own experience, it can be saddening to sense the thoughts of others. If I didn't directly benefit from my hunting, such wretches would overwhelm me with their anguish.

No further information was forthcoming. Command decision time.

"Okay, you two. Out! Breakfast is over, and the kitchen is closed. I need to sleep before I go to work. Nice talking to you, Mercedes or Tatie, or whatever you call yourself. Henri, I will contact you when I get some writing done. Have a nice day, both of you!"

With a little effort, I physically pushed them out the door, then shut and locked it. I checked the stove to be sure there was no burner running, and I went back to bed. Fortunately, I dropped right back to sleep.

When I awoke, it was almost as if I dreamed the whole crazy visit. But the kettle on the burner and the mugs in the sink told otherwise. Strangely enough, they must have taken the instant coffee with them.

Well, no matter: I don't drink coffee and couldn't remember buying it, anyway.

Another thing: it was not a work night! I showered and cleaned my teeth, then went out to hunt some souls.

Souls?

When did my hunting become a search for *souls*? Those crazy telepaths must have really messed with my thinking. I resolved to get back into the mindset that would prove fruitful.

I was hungry and I didn't need another wasted hunt.

NO FEAST

At first, I thought that perhaps my new associates did me some good. That night I was able to skim the meandering nightwalkers and found a quietly distraught, lone woman who was contemplating suicide.

As per my usual procedure, I came up beside her, excusing myself and passing close enough to read her emotions. She was mulling the possibilities of self-destruction in our fair city.

I already knew that guns were used in more suicides than most methods, but this woman had no weapons. She had considered jumping from one of the Interstate bridges, but there was a chance that she would be seen and possibly deterred.

She also rejected hanging or strangling herself. When I caught that, I noticed a pattern. She was discarding one method after another, mostly because she was afraid that if she survived, it would have unpleasant side effects.

Not that that would stop her, but she was easily dissuaded (by herself) from the usual techniques.

I decided to step in.

"You seem so sad, lady. Do you need someone to talk to?" She brightened up, and I was sorry I interrupted her musings.

She was trying to find the least messy way to die. I knew one way that was sure to be nice and clean, but instead I asked her what the trouble was.

She was pregnant and wanted to end the baby's life. She felt she might as well take her own while she was at it. Her nonchalance took my breath away.

But it also took my appetite down several notches. I was never able to stomach even the thought of killing anything innocent: there was just no joy in it. And why take a life that has never truly started? My revulsion for the woman's plan was almost enough to make me lure her for a quick sip, but I could not get past the idea of killing an unborn baby.

I threw up my hands and told her she should just go to an abortion clinic and get rid of the kid. That would solve all her problems, right?

She gave me the weirdest look I have ever received while hunting. Then she drew back and crossed herself. I didn't know whether to laugh or spit at the ground between us.

"Woman, you are batty! You are ready to kill the both of you, but you won't consider just removing the source of the problem? How on earth does that make any sense?" The hunt was ruined; she was beginning to doubt her own intentions. She gave me a sickened wrinkling of her nose and pushed past me.

I stood still for a few moments and watched her disappear into the night, slipping into the first alleyway to the right. Then I walked quietly over to the opening and looked in.

Nobody. There wasn't even an exit or doorway into a home, just a lot of fences and closed garages. She was just gone. I checked around but couldn't find a way out of that alley. Most alleys connect two streets. After all, they were used as places for horse stables, not much more than a hundred years ago.

A little sick to my stomach, I slipped back to the main road, checking to be sure that I wasn't seen.

Searching the rest of my neighborhood proved fruitless, so I ranged out to Lake Pontchartrain. I found a young man seated and staring out toward the water, not moving so much as a millimeter. He looked as if he had died in that position.

"Hey, buddy, what's up? Going for a swim? No? It's kind of late to be looking for little kids..." I said that because it occurred to me he might be a pedophile who watched the nearby playground—and it was sure to provoke him.

The loner turned the most repulsive face I had ever seen towards me. He asked what the hell I wanted with him?

Now, I have seen some oddballs in my life, and even some pedophiles during my disadvantaged childhood, but this was inhuman, the look of pure malevolence. The sort of monster who delighted in his perversions and wanted to share them with me—or anybody else, for that matter.

First I drew backward and considered beating a fast retreat. Then I considered what I had earlier told the two telepaths. If ever our planet needed to lose a predator, it was at that moment.

"Man, you are an ugly cuss, and I bet you know it. Tell me why you are seated here. Trying to look innocent?" He had to be a recluse. I mentally sniffed a bit, to detect his emotions.

I guessed that he was merely annoyed at me for bothering him. I hoped I had touched a nerve with the "ugly cuss" business.

Surprisingly, he wasn't the least insulted. He knew he was ugly, and he was indeed up to no good. I tried a different tack.

"Going for a swim, my good man?" He immediately said no, and if I didn't go away, I was the one going swimming. I chuckled at his gall.

"A long, last swim, no doubt?" The fiend grinned again and stood up. He was a good half-foot taller and was now looking down on me.

I had had bigger hits and began probing for some hint of what was on the menu. From what I could glean, it was going to be a banquet! There wasn't any sin this odd fellow hadn't committed in what seemed to be an impossibly long life.

Problem was, he was not the least bit repentant. Nothing bothered him, not the children he killed, nor the women he had abused, nor the men he challenged and conquered, grinding them into the earth.

One more grin, and he asked me if I had bitten off more than I could chew?

An idea flashed at the back of my mind.

"Say, are you connected to the lady I spoke to earlier? She was a looker, even if a bit torn up, and now here *you* are." I knew I was going hungry for sure, because he smiled even wider.

He asked me if I were mad; how could he have been a woman there and an ugly man here? But by the time I had found the fellow, I had already been chewing on my earlier eerie encounter. If he were tricky enough, he could have easily gotten past me unnoticed.

"Tell me your name, Grandad." He proudly announced that his father had called him Luciel, but usually simply referred to him as "son" or "My son."

"So which is it: Luc or Sonny?" This finally got to him. He was offended and accused me of insolence. There was just the tiniest beginning of sadness in his anger, and I hurried to drink.

His response was another nasty smile, as he noticed that I was drawing on his emotional state. He immediately relaxed and became enigmatic. I detected a sense of cautious hope.

The guy could tell I was baiting and reeling him in, and he found the whole thing amusing. He drew himself up to his full height, and right away, I knew it was an illusion. No one could just grow like that, more than a foot taller.

He was pulling shit on me, so I sneered at his efforts.

"Very clever, but you have mistaken me for a carnival mark. I don't believe everything I think I see. I go by my guts, and my gut tells me you have figured me out. How you know this, I can't imagine, unless you are somehow mixed up with those telepaths in the publishing firm?"

Ugly Man shrank back down to a more manageable size, and I wondered if he was giving in. I drew off a little of his displeasure and tried again.

"So, you know some party tricks. Very clever, Luc! Why don't you take your skills on the road? After all, here in New Orleans, nothing evil and ugly is new, and you can take it from me to the bank."

With that said, the whole hunt went downhill. There was nothing I could say to goad him beyond a little pique over his dignity. I tried again.

"What's with the overblown self-esteem? Can you do what I can? Are you hoping to feast on me? Because you can give it up right now. I take care of myself. You have been caught in Lakeshore Park after hours. A patrol could be along at any moment."

He agreed that I might have him at a disadvantage, but I was working on an incorrect assumption. He wasn't a pervert, and he wasn't a killer or abuser.

"Hold it right there! Your psyche is dripping with the blood you spilled and the pain you have caused."

He countered, telling *me* to "hold it" myself, right there. He had never killed or caused any physical damage to anyone.

When he used *physical*, it caught my attention. That, in fact, was exactly how I worked. Who the Hell was this guy?

And where were the more normal telepaths when I needed them? If this person could work his way around my skills, and could perform even the psychological trick I witnessed, he might be extremely dangerous, indeed.

Suddenly it felt important to call him out. I wasn't frightened, not yet. It was time to end this budding relationship.

"Who are you, really? What is your name?"

He began by calling *me* by name and asserting that he had not lied. His name really was Luciel. I could call him anything I liked, as long as I called him.

Just for a few moments, I was caught off-guard by a flash of purely masculine beauty and power. He saw my reaction. His eyes briefly lit with pleasure, but he immediately returned to the ugly little man I had found on the shore.

Self-preservation kicked in, and I began to retreat.

"Asshole, get away from me! You and I both know I am not getting anything I want out of you. Go away and stay away. I got troubles of my own and I am not adding you into the mix. Go away and do not follow me."

He turned around and went back to staring out at Lake Pontchartrain. His shadow deepened as he did, until he was blacker than the night.

A shade in the dark with no discernible features.

I thought about the vision of male beauty and shivered. Never met anyone with so many tricks. Fighting a maddening urge to return and question him some more, I went directly home.

Although it was a little embarrassing to me, I kept telling him not to follow me. Spoken aloud, but in a low voice, it was like a mantra that made me feel better.

And it got my mind off the guy's amazing stunts.

SAFE AT HOME?

Once I was in my apartment, I nearly fell apart. How could I have let a potential victim turn things around like that?

Obviously, I had a lot to learn about the darker denizens of this historic city on the Mississippi Delta. Now it seemed that it was not so great to live in such a place. A certain Baron Saturday (was it Samedi or Sabado?) came to mind, and I figured I ran across some psycho who was into Voodoo or Hoodoo, or whatever it was.

It didn't matter that he was likely human. It would be quite simple for *anyone* to kill me; I cannot swim. We were never taught, not in school, and certainly not by our mother, who never took us to a beach or pool.

In the very middle of hunting, for me to experience such a strange interlude on the shore of Lake Pontchartrain was looking for an early death. Was I in fact lured by that man, for him to drain me?

Was he a vampire? Or was he just another nutty Goth, who had taken the whole schtick to the maximum? How did he get my name? I rarely use it, and never think about it, except to deal with the government. I don't vote or drive, and I never had any sort of identification, except when I was in the juvenile system, and now a picture ID for paychecks.

Then physical weakness hit me hard; I was starving. I turned my kitchenette upside down before I found a can of tuna. God knows where it came from; I never buy groceries. It practically made me vomit to smell the fish, but I forced myself to eat it.

Feeling a little better, I hit the sack and slept like a baby. When I awoke, I thanked whatever Powers That Be for some peace. It was almost a relief to get up in the late morning and shower for work.

The restaurant was especially hectic, and that meant I could work without thinking. I stayed happily busy and felt even a little put off as closing time drew near.

Once again, Henri was waiting at the back door when I stepped out to head home.

"You again? No time last night to write; I was a little busy hunting." I hoped that would appease him; he might even consider it a sort of research for my book.

I was wrong. He actually took my arm and steered me into the alley.

Henri was furious with me! It felt like a slap in the face, after what I had been through. I was going to tell him to just shut the fuck up, but he cut me off completely.

No. I was going to listen to him, for a change. Ordinarily I would have just turned my back and left him, but I found myself wondering what he knew about my last night's hunt.

His ranting made me think twice before trying to interrupt. My fussy little Frenchie was laying down the law, and I was going to listen from now on.

"You think you are so smart, Little Girl? Let me have my say, and if I am wrong, just speak the word—you know what it is—and my family and I will leave you alone forever."

I never understood the term *gob-smacked* before then. My mouth simply would not obey me. It stayed shut, and for the first time in my life, I was almost cowering before authority. I was simply not in charge.

Henri caught my thoughts and softened his approach, but he still "had his say." I was rooted to the ground, forced to listen to and consider another person's words.

"First off, this is *my* city. You may consider it your hunting grounds, but you should know that you are not the only one who does. It's been a lark, hasn't it? You seek out the wounded and despairing, and then relieve them of their misery.

"Well, I patrol my city, as does my family. We prefer to seek out and help relieve the *pain* of the wounded and despairing. When you arrived and began to eliminate suffering, as you so flippantly call your predation, we felt the darkness seeping in.

"Last night, you let in more darkness. You became the hunted, and you didn't like it, did you? Did you?? You have been marked and will not be safe anywhere in the city except your apartment.

"And you can thank your lucky stars you essentially prayed him away. We were able to seal your door and skylights, so you could get a decent night's sleep."

Unmistakably true! The apartment felt safe, safe enough so I could rest. But it was clear that my assumption about the guy by Lake Pontchartrain had been right.

"Henri, who was that man? I never—" He cut again me off and left me mute.

"You are no longer calling the shots, Little Girl. It's time to return to humanity. You are getting this one chance, and not because you asked for it. You didn't; as frightened as you were, you didn't ask for help. You are so proud of your abilities, as wicked as they are, in the way you use them!

"If you didn't have people praying for you, you would have followed the Evil One to hell, as his servant."

He allowed me to speak.

"Who the fuck *was* that last night? Was he connected to the suicidal woman? And is he one of you? Are you all from Hell, too?"

"You know who it was, who he is. Otherwise you would have been taken in by him with no trouble. The suicidal woman was, and still is, working out problems in her life that have been compounded by pregnancy.

"Emmy, you came awfully close to witnessing a suicide, but your desire to drink in her sadness caught her off guard. Like you, she is a night walker, only in her case, her prey consists of those seeking to pay for illegal sexual encounters. And she considers all customers, male and female."

Henri's explanation of the disappearing woman had me questioning more, so much that I let him use my name without a challenge. I hate my name, because Mommie explained its meaning.

She wanted to hurt me, and she succeeded. At that moment, I wondered—not for the first time—what became of Abby. Her name was given by our father, who was not happy to see me emerge during the birthing.

Mommie thought she had found the love of her life, but she was mistaken. Or maybe she did find the *special* one, but he dumped her after he became the father of twins.

They were counting on a single birth. They could just barely afford one.

Mommie wasn't big on doctors and never bothered to seek prenatal help. She kept the pregnancy secret from the father as long as she could. She wrongly believed that he never wanted children. After all, they were not married, and she was living under his roof at his pleasure, so to speak.

When she finally confessed, he seemed delighted instead of angry. He told her that they would stop at one child.

What nobody knew at the time was that she was carrying twins. We were birthed prematurely, and too small. One or the other of us would likely die, maybe even both.

And dear old Dad was okay with that. He requested that the staff not make "heroic" or special efforts to save both babies, except to feed and change our diapers. Dad had already accepted Abigail as his newborn daughter. He had no name for a twin.

A twin that ultimately survived just as well as the first.

He disappeared from all our lives before Mommie was discharged from the hospital. For the first year, we lived on one charity or another: later she made it clear to local authorities that she was the only one who could care for us. After we were considered stable enough for our mother to manage two babies on her own, we could count on Welfare.

Since our wayward father never returned, Mommie just called us Abby and Emmy. As far as she was concerned, neither of us lived up to the hype of our monikers. Abby ceased to be her "father's delight" just as soon as he left. Emmy and Abby seemed a good match.

Later I learned that Emmy was short for Emily, which was some Latin name that meant "rival" or "crafty." Rival worked for me, since my twin and I were often at loggerheads.

That is, when we were not united against our Mommie.

UNPLEASANT REVELATIONS

So the cat was out of the bag, at least as far as my identity was concerned. It was impossible to keep something so trivial as a name away from the telepaths.

But I had questions, lots of them.

"And how did the streetwalker disappear into thin air? And if you know about last night, why didn't you step in, since he was so dangerous? Was that ugly guy my father? Was he hunting me? Why did he give up?"

Henri laughed. Like the visual of the night before, for just a brief second or less, it sounded like the best music I ever heard. Otherworldly. He shook his head and told me to relax; I should go with him.

He walked me back to his place near the Fairgrounds. Then he told me he was making breakfast, and did I want some?

"Honestly, no. I still would rather find some prey, since I didn't get any last night. And my stomach doesn't do so well with people food."

"Emmy, you would find what you call *people food* much more appetizing, if you bought groceries and prepared real meals. A can of salty fish is hardly good for an empty stomach."

Explanation accepted, but I couldn't face the plate when he set it in front of me. Fruit and some pan-fried potatoes were not what I wanted.

"Another thing, Little Girl. You are done hunting in the streets of my city. We *will* intercept you and prevent any further damage. You can either leave and look for new territory, or you can go back to being just a woman who eats regular food. You certainly lack nothing in cooking skills."

I looked at the plate and began picking at the potatoes. They at least were prepared with oil and spices, giving me something to taste as I chewed them.

"You haven't answered my questions, Henri! Somehow this is your city. I blundered into your territory, and I will have to move on. Is that right?"

"No, my dear. You may stay; you just cannot harm the people or animals who live here. That goes for the dead, too. We sent your mother to find your sister for you."

At first, I was astounded to hear him talk nonsense about "sending" anyone, especially a ghost, anywhere. Then I figured they found her in my memory. But nothing made any sense: who was this dude?

Who were they? Some sort of little Cajun gang, with territory and... what?

I decided to play along, hoping something would start to add up. Instead, he surprised me with his reaction to my unspoken question.

"You don't already know what we are?" Then he shook his head and said he thought it was obvious.

So, even telepaths don't know everything; they could just barely read minds—and souls, apparently.

Then Henri really impressed me. He announced that my sister was surely alive, and they expected to hear from her. Abby did indeed make out very well. She was raised by a wealthy family who even sent her to college. She had no children and was a bit of a loner.

"Like me?" A possible partner?

"No Emmy, not like you. You will learn it as soon as she decides if she wants to reunite with you. Your mother is dealing with her right now, while we speak. The woman you met last night was very good at hiding from you but was not what you consider supernatural.

"That is, unless you want to consider her final destination." Henri was not going to reveal that to me. It was none of my business, what became of her, except where it connected to our conversation. There was not going to be an abortion, nor would there be a suicide.

I had no right to know anything else about her.

"Well, what about that ugly guy? Why was he so, like, magical? At one point he got really tall, at another he turned blacker than the night. And Henri, for about two seconds he became the handsomest man in the world, all power and sexiness. And I don't even like sex!"

"You were afraid of him?"

"He scared the living hell out of me!" Henri responded with a beautiful smile, just as his wall buzzer sounded. He didn't touch the button, but simply said to "come on up."

Not knowing who was climbing the stairs scared me again. I braced myself and pushed the breakfast plate away. The smell was making me sick. Or else everything was making me sick.

I heard the latch click, and Mercedes stepped in, gave me a nod, then hugged her nephew. I thought I would faint from relief.

Then she simply went about making herself a breakfast. She brought it to the table and sat right next to me. Coffee again, and where did she get freshly baked biscuits?

"Feel better this morning? You came close to absolute ruin by Lake Pontchartrain last night . From now on, you cannot approach just anybody you want and still be safe."

My heart sank.

"But how will I feed myself?" The disgust on her face left me a little shaky.

"If you continue to hunt souls, you will eventually meet again with the entity from the lake shore. If so, your next encounter may not end here in NOLA."

While I didn't want to interrupt, I just had to ask.

"Ok, Mercedes, I believe you. But just for my curiosity, why do you call our city NOLA?"

She informed me that there were others like them, and they were in many cities worldwide. She, Henri, and the workers in the printshop were stationed in New Orleans. Henri was in charge; it was his city.

"The rest of us go wherever we are sent. I'm sorry you are confused by the shorthand, but surely you must see and hear it often enough?"

"Wait. I think I get it. Who is in charge where my mother was? Your people who got her God?"

Mercedes said she had been in the prison with Mommie. They were cellmates and went to the chapel together. My mother was sick of being incarcerated all the time but couldn't imagine going back on the streets again.

"Emmy, Kate was prepared to continue her crime spree the moment she was released. She was not able to make it on her own anymore. Her looks were gone, destroyed by methamphetamines, irreparably so. She could only steal, and she wasn't ready to try anything else.

"Your Mommie heard me out and found peace working with the prison chaplain. When the time came for her parole hearing, she was eager to leave and seek a different life. She was becoming a beautiful soul, and other prisoners were not happy for her."

I chuckled.

"I know what happened. She mouthed off about God or morality and got herself killed, didn't she? She said something like that, right? No one wants to hear about religion in jail."

Mercedes smiled and shook her head.

"You're right and you're wrong. There are always people who need to hear about peace and forgiveness. The woman you saved last night is one of them."

Feeling guilty, I had to speak up.

"I didn't save her. I didn't save anybody. She wasn't ready to die, is all it was. I would have drained her if she hadn't been pregnant."

Then I realized what Mercedes had said about Mommie's cellmate.

"*You* were the cellmate? How did you manage that, since you were here at the NOLA office? She must have been in a penitentiary either in Framingham or Springfield, Massachusetts."

Tatie shook her head sadly.

"MCIF(she pronounced it Mc-iff), east of Worcester. All this time you knew how to find her, and you never tried. I had a human ally in MCIF and used her—with her cooperation. She is still incarcerated, as there are hearings going on regarding your mother's death."

My eyebrows shot up enough for me to feel them rise.

"So she has to take the fall for the killer, or at least worked with the one who did the dirty deed? And you let her? Guess you were not so helpful, after all."

Mercedes did not stop shaking her head, but she gave me a sad smile.

"That's all you have to say about the whole affair? Your Mommie lost her life, and another woman will lose her freedom until the day she dies. My human operative will come out okay, but the proceedings will delay her release. She doesn't mind, although right now she is in deep mourning for Kate."

"Telepaths mourn? With all the misery and death there is everywhere, all the time?" Even as I said it, I was embarrassed by my naivete, or at least the sound of it.

"Not long ago you were ready to group us in hell together with your friend Luc..."

"Hey! He's no friend of mine! We don't even know each other. Still don't, I hope." Even saying it made me nervous.

Henri spoke up, and he wasn't smiling.

"Wrong again, Little Girl! Luciel knows you very well. For you, he is the opposite of a godfather."

That caused me to laugh, almost hysterically, until the tears began to run from my eyes. I never really laugh or cry, and the double occurrence frightened me. To regain some self-control, I mouthed off at Henri one more time.

The very last time.

"Henri, you of all people, or whatever you are, should know that we have no godfather, godmother—god anything. Why would you spout such bullshit?" I was feeling better, and even cautiously smug by then.

"You listen to me, Little One! Everyone has godparents, whether or not they know them. And when I say you have the opposite; I am not joking.

"Emmy, you wouldn't let your Mommie have a moment's peace with you, and for good reason. And this week you shut her down when she wanted to tell you her deepest, saddest secret. It is your secret, too.

"Oh, now you don't look so good. Sit back down and put your head between your knees."

I could barely hear Henri, whose voice disappeared into the background of the swirl of racket that I often hear in my dreams and sometimes when I am ready to faint from food-hunger. I did what he suggested, and he went on with what I didn't want to hear.

"You asked if Luciel was your father earlier. That's practically blasphemy, but you were not far from the truth. He was checking on you, to see if you were ready.

"Both your mother Kate and your earthly father were Satanists.

"Your father stepped over the line, showing off for your mother. He called Luciel to himself. I should have said amateur, because your father really didn't know what he was doing. Luc, as you called him, took his time responding. Your father decided he had failed.

"In fact, he succeeded beyond his ability to compre-hend. He got a visit later that night. Your mother was ignorant, almost innocent in her attempts to keep her lover's attention. She learned after your birth that you were promised to the devil.

"In one way, you are like your father. He was such a smart-alec that he thought he could outwit the gran-daddy of all sinners. He decided he could make a pact that would let him and your mother off the hook. He promised his second-born child in exchange for a healthy baby girl."

Even with my head on my knees, I could feel the room rocking.

~~I whispered~~—no, I have to admit it, I whimpered.

"Why would he do that? He deliberately sold me? No wonder my childhood sucked. And he ruined our whole family!"

Mercedes gently lifted my head and shushed me. Henri looked sad as he continued in a low voice.

"Your father did not sell you on purpose. Your Mom-mie was quite a prize back then, and he was doing everything to keep her to himself. If he had her, he would do whatever was in his power to make a better life for his new family. He was ready to marry his lover and raise the child with her."

"Henri, please don't tell me he was ready to eliminate me…" Mercedes stroked my hair and forehead. It felt weird but I had sunk so deep into my grief that I barely noticed.

"Emmy, your father and mother willingly and joyfully followed the pregnancy. You know, they were too poor to consider all the work and the costs of their endeavor. And your mother wouldn't see a doctor until she went into premature labor.

"I know that sounds ignorant, but she wasn't ready to consider anything but her happiness in her situation. Her lover was raised a Christian, but he wasn't beneath praying to God for the good things and cheating everyone—even the devil—to try to avoid the bad. As soon as they were sure of the pregnancy, he had a vasectomy.

"He thought he won. He had a beautiful wife who was thrilled to be carrying his child. Another thing, Emmy, those six months were the only genuinely happy time in your mother's adult life. Tragically, it ended when another baby was born after Abigail.

"Your father guessed then that he was damned, but rather than face it and atone, he deliberately restated the curse and re-directed it back onto you. You would be the baby given over to Satan, after all. He purposefully informed your mother of his pact with hell, and then he disappeared from your lives."

"Where is that bastard now? I will hunt him down—"

Henri cut me off, and once again I couldn't speak.

"You will do no such thing. It is none of your business what happened to your father. It is not for you or your sister, or even your mother to know. Another person's soul belongs only to them. You have no right to know what is hidden within anyone, even your victims. *You never had that right.*"

While I couldn't argue, I wanted revenge. I would punish dear Daddy for all of us.

It would be my consolation before I died and went to Hell.

LIFE SAVING HELP

Living under the protection of the telepaths felt like the work-study programs I had used in college. The only difference was that I was never alone.

Mercedes was with me every minute I did not work. The printshop personnel escorted me to and from the restaurant. They would order a complete meal, and I found it hot and waiting for me when they returned me to the apartment. Sometimes, Mercedes and the men would stay and encourage me to eat.

It took a few days before I began to understand what happened on the shore of Lake Pontchartrain: I had laughed at the Devil and called him my Grandad!

I was just being a smartass, but my mouth got me into deeper trouble than ever before. Funny, how I rarely spoke to people, but twice that night I insisted on performing for my limited public. It was all just an act, but my life could have easily and suddenly ended.

The girl and I never crossed paths again She began to haunt my dreams, and I asked a couple times for permission to find her.

Denied both times. I gave up and the dreams receded.

Jacques and Mathieu from the shop slowly warmed me up to eating again. I really needed help, because I was so accustomed to fasting. Also, they would take me to their work when I began to feel confined.

It pleased me to surprise my keepers! I had classes in desktop publishing, something like a miniature printshop in high school, and was able to handle a few of the smaller tasks. It helped me pass the time and took my mind off hunting.

The feeling of being haunted never left me all the time I stayed in New Orleans. I half expected Mommie to stop by again, but she no longer needed to worry about my fate.

Henri put it simply.

"Kate is entitled to her afterlife, free of connections to Earth. She completed her task; both her daughters are on the right paths."

I pounced on the hint.

"Paths? What happened to my sister? May I know where Abby is?" I finally learned to mind my words. It took a while for me to understand that my life was temporarily on hold, and I lived at the pleasure of my teachers.

Henri gave me a sweet smile and said that I could see her when both of us were ready. Abby could not accept that her vision of Kate was real; she was afraid it was wishful thinking translated into a dream.

Then he changed the tone of his explanation.

"Emmy, your sister is almost as sick as you, only it's physical. We are not omniscient: we don't know if she will die before you reunite."

"Henri, doesn't that just figure? She had everything anyone could ever want, even a loving mother and father. Now we can't have time together. Is that what you are saying?"

Henri spread his hands apart, and I had to understand. Just a few weeks earlier, I would have attacked him, to punish him for adding to my unhappiness. At that moment, I knew I would have paid dearly.

"Emmy, we are still protecting you from Luciel. You are not strong enough to protect yourself. Do you think we are haunting you for our health?"

I laughed at the juxtaposition of those good people haunting and needing to protect their health. Then his words sank in.

"Do I still have to face that Ugly Man? The very thought makes me want to run a million miles in the opposite direction.

"Henri, why won't my mother help protect me?" Then it was the laughter of both Henri and Mercedes that mixed into the loveliest harmony. Better than the sweetest love song.

"What's so funny? She's my mother!" My dinner companions settled down and became serious. Mercedes wanted to say something, and she looked to Henri before she spoke. He nodded and she spoke soothingly to me.

"She has indeed helped you. Everyone has their work to do. Kate raised you as best she could, until you were both safely in somebody's care. She tried to warn you away from Luciel, but life doesn't work out the way we plan.

"You both were needed to talk to the despairing woman. Your callousness was enough to click with her sense of self-pity. She snapped out of it. And, for a few moments, you were genuinely concerned, right after you lost sight of her. Kate herself hid her from your view.

"When you found him, Luciel was already put off by your actions. The two of you goading one another held the whole shop in thrall. We cannot protect anyone who doesn't ask for protection: like Luciel, we can only suggest and present opportunities."

It didn't take a seminarian to work out the meaning behind her simple description of that night. Little by little, I was given small amounts of information that eventually assembled into a picture that was truly scary.

"Henri, will I be safe as long as I remain in your part of the city?"

His flat-out denial stunned me. All the operatives in the world cannot prevent the fall of a soul who is determined to have her own way all the time. Much is demanded of every person, but help is given only when asked.

"Let me correct that. There are some people who are grace-filled and never need to ask for help. Even if they think there is no Almighty God, we are not needed to help them on their way.

"Others never ask and walk their own way to their doom."

"And that is me?" Sickened by the memory of that evil encounter, I was upset that I might have another run-in with the Ugly Man.

Henri shook his head and sighed. I knew I was some-how in error.

"Little Girl, you did ask for help. Every one of those pleas for Luciel to stay away was met by an operative, right up until you made it safely into your apartment. You can understand that we were eager to prevent a disaster. We were encouraged by your thankfulness to what you called the *Powers That Be*.

"But your conversion is not complete. You still are at risk as long as you do not renounce your father's curse. You are still weak enough to live only in the moment, even now feeling lousy and hemmed in by us."

"But Henri—Mercedes! I am grateful. I was so frightened and am still horrified by the possibility of his return."

Both of my companions were keeping something away from me. I could feel it. It was hanging over the conversation like a gloomy fog.

"What? What must I do? Is he here, even now, waiting to strike again?"

Why didn't they just tell me what to say? How the Hell was I supposed to know what to do?

And would I ever see my sister alive, or was she also on a journey of horror? I wanted to go to her and help prevent her own destruction. Perhaps we could join forces!

Henri interrupted my thoughts.

"Abby is saved already. She was given every grace to choose. All the same opportunities that are given to anyone who seeks.

"Emmy, you have never asked; you still are not a seeker. We understand that you were dealt a rotten hand. Many, many people are. Our operatives are all over the world, helping those who ask."

Seeker? What was I doing wrong? At that moment, I felt like a prisoner facing execution at the end of the sentence. I dared not step into the streets, and it was

amazing that there were four operatives ready to protect me from one of their own.

Apparently, all telepaths were not created equal.

DEATH OR DOOM?

No, I did not understand. Somehow the telepaths were able to keep their own kind at bay. While I understood that they could follow me around and somehow protect me, what I could not figure out was why they simply couldn't send the Ugly Man away?

And how could it be that my father was able to curse me? How was I in league with the likes of him and Satanists? It wasn't my fault; I was just a baby. Not even born yet.

We were working at the shop one evening, and all my new companions were together. Perhaps one of the four could direct me to the truth.

"Guys, can we talk? Something is really bothering me about this curse thing. First off, I thought curses were only something in someone's mind. They don't really exist, we just make them happen, right?"

Mathieu looked shocked, but Jacques stayed him with his hand. The look on his face reminded me of Henri. The resemblance had never struck me before that moment.

"Emmy? Do you really believe that?"

Mercedes spoke up.

"Mathieu, she is not ready. Can't you see that? She has not been baptized. Hers will not be of water but fire." Jacques sat back and looked stricken. Matthieu looked away, but Henri stepped in.

Their leader rarely entered our discussions at the printers. He usually concerned himself with editing the older novelettes they were reprinting. He did not address his family, only me.

"Emily, you and Jacques have someone in common. Luciel was dear to him in the beginning. When the evil impulse set in, he chose the better path, and had to leave our fallen brother behind.

"Mathieu was inspired to join him as consolation. We are not all the same age."

That made sense to me. Of course they were not all the same age!

"Well, yeah. Mercedes is the oldest. Before, you told me you all are kin, but now you are all brothers. So you are telling me that Mathieu is the young-est...brother?"

"No, Little Girl, I am the youngest brother. New Orle-ans is my city, but I am still learning the vocation. You are my first difficult case.

"No, please, just listen and learn." I was ready to ob-ject to his assessment of me. Instead, I closed my mouth, swallowed hard, and nodded for him to con-tinue.

"Mathieu and Jacques began their vocation in Israel and Judah, and they had some incredibly challenging cases. There is still a lot of animosity among the religious denominations back there. These days, we have many new operatives in their place."

"Judah? Where in the world is Judah? Henri smiled at my ignorance.

"Israel and Judah were two countries that shared a border. They were the northern and southern kingdoms of the Jews after the death of King Solomon. Is that what you were asking?"

I figured he was teasing.

"Solomon! But that was thousands of years ago!" Henri nodded, completely serious. Suddenly, I believed him.

In an instant, the room ceased to be real to me. My protectors changed completely in my mind. Then I lost the thread of what I was trying to process and found myself waking up on my own sofa.

Once again, Mercedes was stroking my hair, but we were in my apartment. She smiled down at me.

"Back with us now?" I twisted around and Henri, Jacques and Mathieu were still looking concerned. Mercedes continued to speaking soothingly.

"Caught on pretty quick, didn't you? We know that was a lot, and it might be a little too much. We've been trying to take you on this journey in baby steps..." She hesitated, and Henri took over.

"...but you ask a lot of questions. As did your sister. However, she found all the answers she needed in school. Have you ever heard of Assumption College?"

I nodded, because I passed it once or twice in my wandering through Worcester County. I got some disturbing vibes back then. The city was full of churches and synagogues. It was not a comfortable feeling for me, and those neighborhoods were almost devoid of night people, anyway. In that small city, nicer neighborhoods seemed go quiet after dark.

Henri nodded once again. He was trying not to look at me, and I instinctively knew why.

Everything again changed around me. My own apartment did not seem real, or solid, or somehow became unreal, too. It was that same unpleasant feeling from before, when we were all in the print shop.

There was no doubt in my mind that the telepaths did not carry me all the way to my apartment, certainly not through the streets of New Orleans. And that made me wonder just what, or who, had been preventing me from closing in on that college campus.

I sat up and waited for the room to solidify, then I tried again.

"You are angels? The Ugly Man is an angel? Your bodies are not real?"

Mercedes nodded at Henri to continue.

"Call us what you like, but our bodies are as real as yours. As real as your reality. Keep in mind that what you call reality is slightly different for each and every soul in the Universe.

"Don't try to think too much about it. Just trust us. Can you?" I nodded but had my doubts about anyone who might be an angel. After all, if I were cursed, they could think of bad and good very differently than I did.

Henri gave me that smile I was beginning to love.

"Very good, Little Girl! Don't try to over-analyze things just yet. It will eventually come together in one piece—if all goes well."

The last phrase he threw in worried me. I didn't want the darkness to return, especially when I felt so vulnerable. Mercedes stroked my hair again, then stood up.

I was almost overcome with terror.

"Wait! Don't go yet! I mean, I understand that Henri has a whole city to watch, but I feel like I need help now. I still have to face the Ugly Man again, don't I?"

The thought of such a meeting made me want to cry. I never wanted to cry before; I learned not to show any such weakness to Mommie, and it stuck with me since.

I fought back the tears and anxiety and took a deep breath.

"Will you please come with me to face the Ugly Man? Uh, Satan?"

Henri stopped smiling and sat next to me.

"Emmy, you already surrendered to Satan when you willingly began to hunt people for their emotions. Satan is no longer interested in you..."

My throat closed and I choked. There was more, and I was just punched in the gut with Satan!

"But Luciel is more than Satan, who is only one aspect of his evil and something like an underling. Just as we are all answerable to Mercedes. You think of me as the boss, but she is older than any of us, and we look to her to lead us."

That almost surprised me. She never seemed to lead anyone. But she *was* the first to come to the apartment. Then I remembered that she warned me away from Henri and the others.

"Had I been powerful enough to do some damage to Henri? No, wait. To New Orleans?"

Henri looked unhappy.

"You let the Dark One in. Time and time again we have had to eject him. And each time, he had been invited by someone like you. You are the first to actually see him for who he is."

"Well, which one is he? The Ugly Man or the Beautiful Vision I saw for just a second? Okay, you are going to tell me he is both, aren't you?"

Things were getting worse and worse.

"Frankly, I would rather not face the Ugly Man. Seems like that would be tough to handle. Maybe, I could face the Pretty Boy."

All four faces turned to me in alarm. I froze.

Usually, there was always someone who was paying attention to something or someone else. I could see them, just like meercats who always have a lookout, always searching the distance.

Usually it was Henri, but I was feeling guilty about using up all his time and effort. He appeared stunned.

He finally blurted out, "You can't unsay that! And you are not ready!"

Henri sounded very upset, not even angry, as he had been earlier. At first, I wondered why. Then I remembered to ask something that was eating at me from the beginning of our discussion.

"Can any one person, a human, ever be ready? How does anyone knock him back to hell?"

"Emmy, if you only knew. There was one special occurrence, but that knowledge has been withheld from you. Your mother learned it far too late to help anyone but herself."

"Well, what about my sister Abby?" Henri shook his head.

"Abby chose to remain untouchable. She learned what had happened to you, but by that time, she also knew it was out of her hands.

"Now Abigail has done everything she could and can. You will never see her alive again. She cloistered herself and dedicated her life to help you and others like you through prayer."

"I still don't understand why I cannot go to her. We could have a reunion. Maybe the two of us are enough to fight Luciel."

Mercedes nodded in agreement, but then she disappointed me.

"Not just the two of you: your mother, too. But you will face him alone in the flesh. There is no help for it. You must do it yourself. We will try to prepare you, but only you can definitively reject him. None of us are all-powerful, but the word of a human can deflect him, just as you did after your meeting by Lake Pontchartrain."

It sickened me, but if Henri and Mercedes said there was no help for it, that was all she wrote. Those guys wouldn't lie. I knew it by then and know it now. They had been kind enough to break me of my disastrous habit, worse than any addiction a human could have, chemical or behavioral.

I know that now, too. There is no excuse for enjoying the troubles of others, and I not only enjoyed the misery, but I also willingly drank it in and made it my sustenance.

But how was I going to battle such a big badass as Luciel?

I knew a little about Western religions, from pamphlets lying around in a Catholic Charities center for teens, before my placement in the halfway house. I followed up with a visit to the Worcester Public Library. There was so much available, and I grabbed and skimmed several books before I found an illustrated volume about the devil and his minions. It captivated me, but now I know that the pictures were fiction.

There was one interesting chapter, whose heading caught my eye: *Exorcism*. There were a few old movies about demonic possession, but I couldn't watch them. There were just some things that I was never able to watch to the end. It happened enough that I gave up on ever owning a television. Although consumed with interest, I just couldn't follow the programs to their conclusions.

It amazed me that I could read with little problem. Same subject, just in printed form. Some restless anxiety, but I was committed to my day at the Library. I practically memorized one paragraph, because it saddened me, and I didn't know why.

Historically, Christians had all the weapons and armor, so to speak. Jews and Muslims had the birthright as protection, something they inherited from Abraham who got it directly from God. Even so, any of them should find a cleric who specialized in demonology.

The upshot of my one day of research in the library was simple: I had none of those things, those defenses. What's more, I was convinced that I didn't want them or need them. It was easy to dismiss it all as a teenager; re-entering public life was a big enough hurdle without trying to get religion.

Back then, they were like fairy tales. I happened upon them during the worst time of my life; they were no help for me. How could I know that all that stuff about exorcism was true? That I would one day find out for myself?

And I couldn't just beg for such graces at the last minute and expect them to be mine, not completely.

I was doomed to face the Ugly Man alone.

PRETTY UGLY

It ate at me all night and into the next day. I kept an eye out for Luciel, even when I was with my mentors. There was no way I would face him alone.

Fortunately, Jacques and Matthieu were there to escort me to the restaurant and would return to take me back home afterwards. I knew I was safe with them, and work would keep me busy and with other people in the meantime.

Still, I was distracted for half the workday. I should have known that others might notice that my head was not in food preparation, even though my hands automatically followed through, as usual.

I thought I had it covered, and I was used to putting on a front. This day my luck ran out. Our short-order help would never dare question me about, well, about anything. I never abused them, but they feared me, just the same.

A fog had settled on my brain, and I was just pushing ahead, when a cook passed a note from the door to the kitchen.

My heart sank: Boss wanted to talk to me. I handed my fancy plating job over to the cook, who winced, nodded sympathetically, then turned away.

The owner and I stepped out into the alley.

He ventured to touch my arm, but he quietly and sincerely spoke about my health. He wanted to know what was bothering me. My work was still high quality, but I was burning and cutting myself and staring off sadly into the distance.

What had happened to his cocky young chef who didn't bother to acknowledge the accolades to her work in the local media and internet reviews?

"Family problems. I'll get over it." Boss then took my hand. His was just as roughened from kitchen work as mine. Immediately, it comforted me more than his kind words.

He looked me in the eyes, his face full of compassion. Something entirely new for me. I barely heard his apology.

"I am sorry. You never mentioned any family. You mean the two guys who walk you to and from work?" He lowered his voice as he asked. I never thought about Jacques and Mathieu escorting me; I just accepted it, as part of my protection.

"If my work is suffering, I guess I owe you an explanation. I had just learned my sister was still living, but, um…"

The boss stopped me.

"You don't have to tell me anything more. It's none of my business, but you seem so preoccupied. Why don't you just connect with her? Oh, right. You don't have a cell, do you?" I had never bothered to get a smartphone, or even to connect the landline in my apartment. No one to call.

I shook my head and turned to go back to work, but he insisted.

"Wait. You can search on my iPhone. I don't mind; take it. This screen is the search engine. You type in her name and address or approximate whereabouts.

"Really, I trust you. Go ahead. You can at least get started. Maybe it will help."

He handed me the phone and left, offering to give me privacy. He would be on the floor with the diners, when I wanted to return it.

It took a minute for me to type out my sister's full name, because my fingers seemed fatter than I thought they were. Once I got that in, a page of choices came up. I saw the Worcester Telegram and Gazette's site.

The same newspaper that was there when I lived in the county. I tapped that selection, and a brand-new obituary came up.

There was a headshot of a nun in an old-fashioned getup—stiff, white cloth surrounding her face, but she was certainly my twin. Her eyes were not lifeless like mine had been in the mirror. She was from a "cloister of contemplative" sisters, and that sounded right.

There would be no calling hours and only a private funeral in the convent's chapel.

Abby was already dead. Died the night before, probably after my mother stopped in. I should have guessed. Now there was no one who could help me. And even if I had contacted her in time, there would have been no way to get together. Cloistered nuns deliberately shut themselves off from the world, sometimes even family.

I knew that much from the Catholic Charities pamphlets.

What Henri had said began to sink in. I would not have been able to even enter the abbey. Not while I was marked by Satan or Luciel himself. It felt like being unfairly backed into a corner, but the truth can hurt.

"Hey, how did you make out?" Boss took back his phone before I could figure out how to hide the obituary. His eyes popped when he saw the picture.

"Looks just like you, except in the eyes. Actually, lately your eyes have been looking better. You've been eating well?" I waved him away and muttered a thank you.

I needed some time to process what I saw. He spoke once more, his voice softening considerably.

"Oh, I am so sorry! Now you really are alone."

That last declaration was practically whispered, and his voice went melodious as he dropped the local drawl. Without looking up, I told him that I have always been a loner, but I had hoped my twin was still alive.

"Come. You need a hug. We can work through this." Then I noticed the smooth hands with perfectly manicured nails and smacked them away. Alarm bells filled my head.

"Since when do you get manicures? You!! Get the hell away from me!" I crossed my arms and stepped as far from him as I could. My back bumped against the dumpster, and I knew the property was surrounded by a stockade fence.

There was no way out, except through the restaurant. I tried to grab at the phone, but it melted away before my eyes. It didn't matter where it went, anyway. My manager would be far too busy to even remember it until later.

And was it ever really there in the first place?

The warm smell of male musk filled the air around me. That was a misstep on Luciel's part; it was simply an inoffensive body odor for me.

My supervisor was right when he had suggested I was asexual.

I spat as hard as I could, but my unnaturally handsome assailant deliberately let it hit his face. He leered: didn't flinch or wipe it away. Instead, he stuck out an improbably long tongue and used it to lick away my saliva. Then he smacked his lips and came even closer, leering right in my face.

There was no way to push further backwards; Luciel blocked any path to freedom. He seemed to fill all my senses. The city around us evaporated.

"What's wrong, my little love? I can give you what you've always wanted." Pretty Boy was moving closer. And I knew what he *wanted* me to want.

"Not what I want any more!" At least I could talk, but I felt hopelessly outmatched. Luciel spoke easily and his voice was all I could hear; even the sounds of the city were gone.

"I choose you, my princess, out of all the women of New Orleans, this charming city that overflows with my witches and worshippers. You and I can feast until the end of the world; then we can rule the next."

Instead of laughing, I sniffed bitterly.

"Yeah, and then what? An eternity of regret? What sort of kingdom is that? You can have it, but you can't have *me*." Desperately, I tried to remember what the telepaths were saying about getting rid of him.

The Pretty Boy switched back to the Ugly Man.

"Your friends cannot help you, and they know it! They even told you that you are mine for the taking. Listen to what I offer—my servants shall wait on you, hand and foot. Think of the luxury of it, especially after a lifetime of isolation!"

That thought frightened me more than anything I could imagine. He was getting it all wrong and needed to shut up and let me think.

"No! I still want to reconcile with my sister and mother, even if it is after my death. And you of all, uh—entities—must know I don't enjoy life. So why live forever?

"Besides, what is left after the end of the world? We would watch the beaches disappear and the mountains wear down. Maybe the Earth will become nothing but ocean, with everyone who ever lived resting under the seafloor. Then what?"

Luciel grabbed at my description, becoming a smiling Pretty Boy again.

"So much more and you can witness it all! It will be magnificent; I can promise you. There is nothing that isn't beautiful in my Father's creation. Look at me; I am one of His firstborn children. His favorite from before Time.

"If you come with me, my love, you will live beyond Time itself. And I can show you other worlds; we can watch them as they form and develop and disintegrate.

"Think of all the souls that will be ours for the taking!"

Holy fricking shit! That was exactly what I didn't need, and he wouldn't accept my word.

Then, the thought of such an awful eternity, at least until the end of the universe, suddenly made me very calm and almost puzzled. I never before thought about other worlds, or even an afterlife. There was so much left for me to learn on Earth, about regular people and how normalcy might feel.

With that thought, that wish for just a simple life of daily work and some fellowship with those around me, my ego completely deflated.

"No. Not for me. I was absolutely wrong; it's sick to drink other people's emotions. It was a satisfying experience for someone who was miserable to begin with. But this last day, while I was sad and mopey over being separated from my family... From my mother and my sister, both who love me..."

His breath was warm and sweet but still disgusted me. The Pretty Boy whispered right in my face.

"But you don't love them. They are not for you, and if they ever were, they are now gone. They cannot come back to life to help you. You can help yourself! Come, we shall rule this city and all my worshippers, for a start. Think of ruling all of New Orleans and then the world!"

At that moment, I didn't know who was showing me what I imagined, but suddenly I was just a tiny dot, infinitesimally small in that alley. Then New Orleans became a single speck on the bottom of a geographic map, and the vision backed up until I saw North America become multi-colored smears under white clouds on a blue planet. The blue planet I had seen in NASA pictures. That, too, was sucked back to nothing in an infinity of stars.

Gripped by vertigo, I began to panic.

"Stop right now! You are making me sick to my stomach. I don't want to rule anyone except myself. And it's been tough enough learning how to do that." Heck, I wasn't sure I managed that much.

Pretty Boy was staring down at me, unconcealed disdain in his otherwise beautiful face. I knew then that no human woman could ever be grand enough for the likes of him, even if anyone wanted to try.

I recognized the hate: the same hate I had had for other people. He would swallow me up, along with all the souls he had duped along the way to our meeting on the shore of Lake Pontchartrain.

And he would continue to consume souls, right up until there were no more to be teased along. All the misery in the world, but he wasn't getting mine.

The sadness of it all nearly overwhelmed me.

The struggle was wearing me down, and I fought to regain control. The new me, the one that was trying to learn from and please the telepaths, fell away.

The wiseass know-it-all who had nothing left to lose took over.

"All right, Luciel! Yeah, I said your name. If you can say mine, I can say yours. Right? Your visions are Somebody else's grandeur, and you understand that better than I do or ever will.

"Get over yourself!

"I don't know what you did to my mother, but she got away from you, didn't she? And you are wrong about my family. Mercedes and the others said that Mommie, and now Abby, are praying for me. They might even be right here with us, even though I can't see them.

"My father did this to us, and I may never figure out what happened to him. I should pray that he got away, I know, but I am not ready to forgive him for the horrific mess he handed me. Not right now, anyway. I am just one cursed person who never had a chance to live an ordinary, human life.

"Until now. And I want that life, the one I didn't get yet. The grief over my sister will come and go. I never realized that I missed my mother and sister all these years. But I still want to feel that sadness just because it's real: they were mine, even though I thought otherwise."

Then it was the Ugly Man who stared back at me until I couldn't stand him any longer. He was unattractive all right, but I never saw human ugliness that made me feel the revulsion I felt at that moment.

Then Luciel made another mistake: once again, he stepped right up to my face and growled loud and deep, to scare me, I guess. The sound filled, then resonated through, the alley, but I simply stared back, indifferent.

I was not frightened at all. To me, growling was the sound of a scared dog, a miserable animal. Even more tragic, a wounded creature.

All of them, just like me.

What's more, I was sick to death of both Ugly Man and Pretty Boy. Tired of Luciel and how he was tearing me down. I wanted him to go away and not come back. He could see it, and he spoke quickly.

"Don't say it, woman. You will die if you do."

"You are right, I guess I will die. I never thought about it before. Maybe I have you to thank for that. Ready or not, I am saying it now.

"To Hell with you, Luciel! I condemn you; go back to where you came from. You cannot have my soul. My father had no right to offer me to you, and I am taking myself back. I quit the part of me that belonged to you, so go away. Do not return, because I will say the same each time. Go back to Hell and stay there, away from me."

I was frantically trying to think of the word that people use when they send the Evil One away. There was something Catholics recite, but what was it? I wanted to say it to Luciel, but when I stopped for a moment to gather my wits, he was gone. Gone too, was the musky aroma and the claustrophobia of being imprisoned in the alley.

"Did you mean *renounce*?" Henri was laughing happily at me. "I think Luciel got the message. He left you and he won't be back in our city for a while."

Still dejected, I felt tears burning my eyes.

"You mean I didn't get rid of him for good? Because I didn't know the right word?"

"It's not about the right word, Emily. It's the right intention, and you have the right intention. Still, it is okay to cry; you've just been through a taste of Hell. Few people are up to facing him the way you did. Especially knowing what you know.

"Exorcists have great faith and years of training, and you have neither. But you do have your soul back, and you know how to protect it. And our city is safer now. Go back to work and finish your shift."

The iPhone sat in the dirt at my feet, so I retrieved it and wiped away the dust. When I looked around again, I was alone.

Inside the door, as if nothing had happened since we talked, my manager was waiting with a worried look.

I handed the phone back to him; he reached up with a fancy cloth napkin and wiped my tears. He must have guessed what I found on his iPhone.

"I am really am sorry about your loss. I feel like a jerk for leading you to it on the internet." I shook my head, smiling, but the tears kept coming and I couldn't talk.

Boss sent me home on a personal day; he would take over my position for the night. When I left the building, no one was waiting to see me home. What's more, it felt strange to leave work before sundown. The sky was all different shades of pink, orange, yellow, and blue.

Before that moment, I never bothered to notice the New Orleans sunset—or sunrise. I walked to the apartment building and let myself in. My legs were still wobbly from both emotional stress and muscle fatigue, so I took the elevator.

Once inside the apartment, I could still see the different colors through the skylights. I went into the bathroom and washed my face with cold water. The thought of going out to shop for supper needed more energy than I had, so I decided to make some tea and watch the sky finish changing colors to dark blue.

I stopped short at the bathroom door.

Supper was laid out, nice and hot: lobster tail and pan-fried potatoes, with fruit for dessert. I didn't thank the empty room out loud, but I knew they heard me, anyway.

I ate with a real appetite, maybe from all the crying. Then I changed my clothes and headed out toward the printshop.

There was still a lot of work to do; I wanted to publish my story.

JJ Leander lives in the
Southern Tier of Upstate New York.

She has a husband and three cats.

You can contact her at

jjleander54@gmail.com

Made in the USA
Middletown, DE
15 November 2020